To Ali,,
Thank you
for the love!
Dani
René xo

THE SINS OF SEVEN

OBEY

DANI RENÉ

WARNING

In a world of secrets, where sins are hidden from sight, people live their lives hoping that those around them never know what desires they conceal. The darkest needs, those that taunt just below the surface. Those they hide in the deepest recesses of their minds. Those things they don't admit to. The things they don't talk about. That's what this series touches on. You may find some of the subject matter disturbing, you may even look away, cringe, and gasp. But that's why I wanted to write these seven couples. These couples came to me with their confessions and I obeyed their need to have their stories told. The dark, depraved, the taboo. The things we may find tempting, alluring, and may even be turned on by it. That's what I wanted to write.

Each story is an interconnected standalone, delving into the relationship of the couples you'll meet. There will be sex, there will most certainly be foul language. And there will DEFINITELY be taboo subjects covered.

The Sins of Seven revolves around seven couples who are so different in nature, in what their likes and dislikes are. They're each unique in desire, in their personalities, and even in the way they try to show affection. They don't love. At least, they don't think they do, they don't believe they're worthy of it.

Each story will make a point of focusing on one of the seven deadly sins.

Greed, Pride, Lust, Gluttony, Sloth, Wrath, Envy.

Although they'll be released in their own order, you'll be able to tell which sin, follows which couple and their journey to possibly find their happily ever after.

Please heed this warning.

This is a dark romance, suitable for mature audiences, 18+ ONLY. Strong sexual themes and violence, which could trigger emotional distress, are found in this story. Certain scenes are graphic and could be upsetting to some. Proceed with caution. Discretion is advised.

Each of us is born with a box of matches inside us, but we can't strike them all by ourselves.

Laura Esquivel

To the women who love the dark.

Who submit and relinquish control.

Be careful who you give that gift to,

not all are worthy of your submission.

To ALL women out there,

I want you to remember one thing,

no matter how broken you feel,

you are strong and beautiful.

Don't let ANYONE tell you otherwise.

PROLOGUE

GIANA

It's been weeks since I saw him. Since the moment I laid eyes on the tall, dark and handsome man, I knew I wanted him. My memory is crystal clear. It's him. It's always been him, only I can't go to him and tell him who I am, so I watch him from afar. He walks into the store with his briefcase in hand every day, dressed in an Armani suit that is tailored for him. I know this because there's no secrets between us. At least, there never used to be.

Elijah Draydon.

Thirty-six-year-old billionaire with a seemingly

perfect life. At least, that's what it looks like from where I'm standing. With eyes the color of gold, dark hair that's tousled in such a way I wonder if he fucks just before he walks into the store. And lips that curl perfectly into a Cupid's bow. Full, pink, and delicious.

His five o'clock shadow is barely there, the dark dusting just visible, making sure my thighs squeeze together in that needy way I'm sure most women do when they look at him. Everything about him screams sex; he exudes it like it's part of his personality. I have no doubt that when he sheds that designer suit, it's exactly what he's good at. Making women come so hard they forget their own name. I just wish I could be one of those again. I was once, only he doesn't know it. He won't recognize me because I don't look the same. I've changed my hair, I no longer have those god-awful braces, and I've grown into a woman. Years have passed, and even now when I look at him, I recall every moment his fingers touched my body, and the way his lips would devour my cunt.

Each morning, I serve his coffee and at every lunch time I make sure his Caesar salad is free of croutons. But he doesn't know who I am, he doesn't recognize me.

My job at Mocha Coffees is only my day job. It's at night that I see Eli in a completely different light. In the way I remember him.

When he walks into the nightclub where I work the bar, that's when he's in his element. Dressed in dark jeans and a smart dress shirt, he still looks as well put together as he does in the daylight hours, the only difference is what he's drinking, and the entertainment he enjoys.

Beautiful women flock to him while he sits at the bar. Out of all the hundreds of plastic Barbie dolls that drape themselves over him, he'll choose one to take home. I've heard stories about his dungeon. I've also heard about his penchant for rope, pain, and choking.

"Good morning, Giana."

The deep rumble of his voice is enough to have my panties wet. Glancing up, I find the man in question standing before me with a smirk on his face. "Good morning. The usual?" He nods, then drops those golden eyes to his phone. As I make the Americano, I steal glances at his fingers, remembering how they felt pleasuring me.

Clearing my throat, I set the cup down. "Thank you." Another smirk. He offers me the note and grabs the mug. "Keep the change." With that, he leaves me staring at his beautiful form. *One day, Mr. Draydon. One day soon.*

ONE

ELIJAH

"Eli, you can't spend your life grieving. Find someone new. Move on." Her imploring gaze haunts me. Her eyes, that used to shine with life, with love, are now a faded gray. Her hand is cold, ice to my warm touch.

"I love you. You'll always be in my heart. Why would I give it to someone else?" It's the same conversation we have over and over again. We run in circles. We've been doing it for six months of her being in here. She forgets so easily these days. Sometimes, she'll look at me and I know she doesn't even recognize me.

As we turn the corner, I notice her again. A young girl. She can't be more than seventeen with golden skin, and her big brown eyes seem empty. Almost as if she's lost all will to live.

16

It's sad to see someone so young already so haunted by life.

"Look at her Eli," my sweet wife whispers, her throat closing up with emotion as she points out the girl I've been blatantly staring at. "Isn't she just beautiful?" Her voice is almost faraway but I nod to appease her. I don't want to let her know I can see what she's doing. I'm way too old for starting over, too broken to find someone for love, but perhaps I can fix her. Make her feel again. Light up her dull brown eyes.

"She's lovely," I respond to my wife.

"Why don't you talk to her? You're so good with people."

I don't reply. It hurts that she's palming me off on someone else and she's not even dead yet. The thought grips my chest painfully. Agony slices through me, and I find it difficult to breathe.

"Don't be silly. She's just a girl." And even though I want to go to the girl, to talk to her, to hear what she sounds like, I don't. Raquel knows my need. She's been through it all. Seen me when the craving took over. The hunger. The lust. And even now, as her life drains from her body, she's still my submissive. My toy. Doing what any good slave would do, making sure that once she's no longer here, that I'll move on without regret.

I sit beside my wife under the hot sun and wonder where my life is about to lead when she takes her last breath. I don't know. Acceptance is not in my blood, not when I have to come to terms with losing the one woman who broke me as much as I broke her. And in those pieces, we found completeness.

The door to my office opens, dragging me from the memory. When I glance at the little woman who's just walked in, I find myself wanting to lose my shit, but I sit back and wait.

"Daddy," she utters in that syrupy sweet tone, but I shrug it off. When I shove the photo over the desk to her, she blanches, all that makeup couldn't cover up her guilt. "I-I..." Her wide eyes flit between me and the photo she sent Oliver.

"What the fuck did you think would happen if you acted like a slut?" Growling, I slam my fist on the desk, sending a loud echo through the room.

"I didn't mean—"

"Like fuck you didn't mean to. You spread your fucking legs for that asshole? Was I not good enough anymore?" The rage in my tone is palpable. This little whore thinks she can use me. Thought I wouldn't find out she's fucking my partner, calling him Daddy too.

"Daddy, please?"

Her pleading only serves to piss me off further. "You've lost the privilege of calling me that. Pack your shit and get out."

Big doe eyes, glistening with tears, peek at me under dark lashes. She knows better than to argue. Rising from the chair, she heads to the door. It's almost time to go home so she can fuck right off and never come back.

As soon as the door clicks closed, I sit back and realize I've just lost a toy I was enjoying. Her love of rope was intoxicatingly sexy. When I choked her long, slender neck, her cunt would squeeze my dick so hard I would come instantly.

Sins are evil. They taunt us, bringing us to the point of madness, leaving only shells behind. An empty carcass of the person they devoured. Mine? Lust. Sinful, vengeful, and driven by desire. Even though I play with many toys at a time, I don't consider it cheating; it's merely filling that void left by the one woman who I was meant to spend forever with.

"Eli," the rumble of my partner, and best friend of thirty-odd years drags my attention away from sending my toy away. The one who worked for me, my fucking assistant who I could order to suck my dick at any point I needed it. "Did you just fire Brie?"

"Yeah."

"Any reason why?" he questions, knowing full well why I did it.

Lifting my gaze, I pin him with an incredulous stare. "Do you really want me to get into this with you right now?"

"Yeah, I do."

"You were fucking her behind my back and you're asking why I'm firing her? Look in the mirror, smart ass. You could have afforded me with asking permission."

He looks at me guiltily, but immediately shakes it off as only my best friend would. We've known each other far too long to let a piece of ass get in the way. Oliver is someone I respect, admire, and ultimately, he's like a brother to me. He is however, very different than me. A sadist who enjoys doling out punishments and pain. He also has a penchant for both sexes. Males and females fall over themselves to kneel for him.

"Her cunt was hot and tight. What can I say?" he says, shrugging and stepping further into my office.

"I know it was, that's why I kept her in the office," I confess easily, earning me a chuckle.

"Look, I didn't know you had feelings for her," he retorts with an arched questioning eyebrow.

I don't do feelings. I play. I use. I taunt and tease. There's nothing outside of that world. I'd given up on love when I lost my wife. There was only one girl who ever gave me a run for my money on that, and I walked away from her. When I left her in that room, I told myself she didn't want me and I forced myself to believe it. In my mind, I was convinced she used me as much as I did her. It was easy to push people away. For me to spend my time alone, detached.

Pushing off the chair, I head to the bourbon cabinet. I call it that because it's the only alcohol I keep in my office. My father once told me businessmen conduct better meetings over a shot of whiskey. The crystal tumblers I set down on the counter glisten in the dimly lit office. It's past working hours, and as the sun settles on the horizon, I wonder if it would be a good idea to visit Seven Sins tonight. I pour two shots of the Michter's Celebration Sour Mash I bought a month ago. It's one of my favorites, and I savor each and every drop. When I hand one to Oliver, he glances at the bottle and nods *thanks*.

"Did you want to head down to Seven Sins with me?" I question, before taking a long sip of the thick, decadent liquid. It burns its way down my gullet like a silky poison.

"Do you want to share a tight little slut? Or are you wanting one for yourself?" he counters before downing the drink in one easy gulp, and pouring himself a second shot.

"Let's find one to share. I want an innocent. One who's not in the *pool*. Someone we can corrupt and defile." My mouth curls into a dark and sinful smile; that's what I heard one of my toys at the club once tell her friend about my lips.

He nods, an evil smirk on his face, and I know my best friend will be up for a fun night. "Meet you at eight," he grunts, downing the three fingers of whiskey easily without even a wince. Pushing off the chair, he leaves me in my office to let my mind roam over what we're going to do tonight.

It's no secret in the club that we're up for sharing, hell, we're notorious for it. What's got me even more excited is knowing I'll see *her* tonight. The pretty brunette with those soulful eyes. Deep and endless pools of brown that simmer with desire. I am reminded of the girl I left long ago. I should have taken her with me. But in my grief, I walked away and now I regret it.

I may not be able to go back in time, but deep down all I can do is hope she's okay. That she found her way in life. Sighing, I know I need to focus on the present and leave the past behind me. The brunette, Giana, is on my mind as I leave my office. I wonder if she'll want to be owned and used.

"Hello, Eli." Her voice is sultry and sensual as usual. My sweet intoxicating beauty from the coffee shop smiles at me with those pretty brown eyes that seem to beg me to take her. She just turned twenty-three. I overheard her telling her friend about the party she had.

Her appearance here in the club is vastly different to her little coffee shop outfit. "Hello, Giana." My tone is low as I lean in and pin her with a gaze. She blushes furiously. "I'll have a bourbon, make it a double. It's been a long day." She nods as I settle on the stool at the bar. The low beat of the music thrums through my chest and the haunting voice of Marilyn Manson comes through the speakers. *Sweet Dreams* are definitely what I'd like to give little Giana. A deep bass vibrates through the club as the curtain opens, and I'm met with a blonde toy bound to a pole on the stage.

As her Dom walks onto the platform, Giana sets the glass down on the bar beside my arm. "Here you go, I've poured you a triple since you said it's been a long day." Turning to regard the woman who's clearly gripped my attention, I offer her a thankful smirk. The crystal tumbler glints under the low lights, but my gaze is locked on the beauty before me. I wonder how she'd look writhing between Oliver and I while calling me Daddy and him Sir. As much as I love sharing a beautiful girl with my best friend, something about this toy makes me territorial.

"Do you enjoy breaking the rules, Giana?" I question, before taking a long sip of the amber liquid. I normally drink a dry gin and tonic when I'm in here, but tonight I felt like something heavier. Something darker.

"Sometimes," she murmurs. "It depends on the person I'm breaking them with." If that wasn't an invitation, I don't know what is.

"How about you join me tonight? I'll show you how to shatter all the fucking rules," I offer, draining the glass. Before Giana can answer, the blonde on stage cries out in pleasured pain. We both drag our attention to see the Dom whipping her beautiful cunt.

"Do you do things like that?" she questions in a soft, raspy tone.

My head snaps back to the brown-eyed goddess I'd love to whip until she's coming all over me.

"It depends on the person I'm with," I quip, throwing her words back at her with a deep growl.

"And if that person happens to be me?" she asks. Her head tips to the side with a quizzical expression on her face. I'm about to answer when Oliver strolls up beside me, settling himself in the vacant seat.

"Bourbon, pretty girl," he orders gruffly. Turning to my best friend, I notice he's a bit worse for wear.

"What's crawled up your ass?" I question, before turning back to watch Giana pour two triples into the tumblers she set aside.

"You remember that asshole, Fredericks?" he growls. I nod. "Well, he just called. He wants me in court tomorrow at seven."

I knew that would happen. Chuckling, I lift the glass as soon as my new toy sets them down. With a wink, I offer her a nod, hoping she'll understand we need space. I'm pleasantly surprised when she does pick up on my silent signal and heads over to the far end of the bar to serve other customers.

"I'm more than happy to take a rain check, man," I inform him, knowing that he takes court seriously. He never stays out late if he's got an early morning appearance. Neither do I for that matter.

I knew I had to move on from mediocre jobs and that's when I started working with Oliver. He agreed to hire me as long as we didn't let our friendship get in the way. At work we were colleagues, after hours we were best friends, brothers. I knew I wanted to work for the infamous Mr. Michaelson. Over the years, I'd been with every other company. I looked up to him. Watching his career progress, the man is as ruthless in a courtroom as he is in the dungeon. When I first saw him walk into Seven Sins, I had been working with him for a year. It brought us closer together, knowing that we both had a penchant for the darker side of life.

The first time we shared a girl was when he took Nathan Ashcroft and me on as trainees. He taught me about delivering pain, just the right amount to draw pleasure from the female form. He knew Raquel. He introduced us. Always intuitive with what is going on around him. And since then, he's been a brother, a mentor, and a business associate. He announced me as partner to his firm after my fourth year. Being a few years older than me, you'd think the man would make sure I knew it, but he treats me as an equal, and that's earned him my respect.

"I better go, or I'll be here all night tempted by

the beautiful women and men. See you in the office tomorrow. And—" He leans in, and his gaze casts over my shoulder to Giana. "Don't be late."

I don't know how he does it. How he knew that she's going to be beneath me tonight, but once again, he floors me.

"I won't," I respond quietly. Sipping on my drink, I don't meet his gaze that seems to be burning a hole through me. Once I set the glass down, I finally meet his gray eyes. He merely smiles as he saunters out of the club, leaving me to plan my night with the pretty bartender.

TWO

GIANA

He's been sitting there watching show after show, and with each of them, I notice him sip the drink I poured him slowly, as if savoring it. And I know it's his way. When he's about to play a scene, or take home a toy, he doesn't get drunk, ever.

When I pretty much offered myself to him earlier, I thought he was going to take me up on it, but Oliver appeared, had a quick drink, and then left.

I have another hour to go on this shift, and all I keep thinking about is kneeling for this man, having him bind me to a pole and whip me until I'm screaming his name. And we all know that I definitely know his name.

He rises from the chair and turns toward me

with his signature smirk on that incredible mouth. "I'm heading out," he murmurs over the bar, slipping something toward me on the mahogany surface. "If you're interested in breaking any rules, you'll need this."

I don't look away, keeping my gaze on his; I reach for the plastic card and watch as he makes his way to the exit. Once the door shuts and he's out of my line of sight, I take a look at the card beneath my fingers.

A sleek silver rectangle the size of a credit card. On the top, centered in dark ornate lettering, are the initials *E.D.* I flip it over. There's an address printed in a generic type. No phone number, just the three lines of a local home; my heart catapults into my chest.

It's been so long since we've been close. Since his fingers have brought me to orgasm that the tingle between my thighs intensifies at the thought of once again feeling him. Every nerve in my body tells me to go for it. I have nothing to lose. Slipping the card into my pocket, I continue the rest of my shift with a smile on my face and my belly flip flopping with nerves.

When I pull up to the gates, there's a small intercom I can access from the driver's window. I push the button once and hear the buzzing from the speaker. A click. Then the gates slide open with ease.

The anxiety flutters in my stomach, and I wonder if he'll recognize me from his past. Pulling up the drive, the house comes into view, stealing my breath. Three levels of incredible beauty. Lit in a soft orange glow from the drive and the windows, I take in the monstrosity that is the Draydon Mansion.

Once I kill the engine, I exit the car on shaky legs and head toward the door. Before I can knock, it swings open, and I'm met with a lady who looks to be in her late forties. She's incredibly beautiful with a tight bun at the back of her head. Her makeup is immaculate, better than mine, and she offers me a nod. I take in her appearance, noticing she's dressed in a black and white uniform.

"Hello, I'm—"

"Giana? He's in his office," she says, gesturing to the right as she steps aside and allows me to enter. The warm smile on her face puts me at ease for a moment, but as soon as I take in the interior of the home, I'm speechless. The dark décor reminds me of an old Victorian castle with the dark reds, blacks, and grays. There's a navy and purple modern artwork that hangs on the wall at the entrance, and smaller ones along the walls which seems out of place with the rest of the décor, but even so, it's breathtaking.

Two large vases both filled with red roses fragrance the room with their alluring scent and I can't help inhaling deeply. I recall the day Elijah walked into my hospital room with a single red rose he'd picked in the gardens. My most prized possession. Red for lust and a rose for love.

The maid, who hasn't told me her name, leads me toward a drawing room, or is it called a living room? There aren't any sofas, only two wingback chairs and a long dark wooden table that runs almost the length of the room.

"Wait here," she says, leaving me standing in the abandoned room and shutting the door behind her. My eyes roam around the room, taking in the paintings, large fireplace, and the windows that overlook the back garden. A small patch of grass is lit up by lamps outside, which allows me to make out the flowerbeds just outside the windows. I feel him before I hear him, then the lights in the room dim to almost full darkness.

"Hello, Giana." The sensual timber of Elijah's voice comes from somewhere in the room, but I can't see him. "I'd like you to strip for me. I want to see what beautiful lingerie you have hidden under those clothes." The order is veiled in a soft, sensual whisper.

"Eli—"

"I didn't ask you to speak. I asked you to take your clothes off," comes his fluid response. No nonsense. Commanding. This is what I wanted, what I've craved for far too long.

Nodding, I tug the T-shirt, which is part of my uniform, over my head. The pink lace bra I'm wearing molds to my B cup breasts. My nipples are hard from exposing myself like this to a man I've thought about every day since I was eighteen and he walked out on me.

Unbuttoning the jeans I'm wearing, I slip them down my legs and step out of the fabric, leaving it on the floor beside me. I want to ask him why he's doing this. I also want to know if he's going to fuck me, but all I can think about is the fact that I can't see him and he can see me practically naked.

"Good girl. Now, I want you to climb onto the table in front of you. Kneel like a submissive would. You know how to do that, yes?" he questions and I nod. "Good. Your pert little ass will perch on your heels, your palms on your thighs, and those pretty brown eyes closed."

Every word of his instruction drips with desire and dominance. A deadly combination. It is cloaked with lust which matches my own. Obeying him, I slip onto the table and sit back.

My hands, as he mentioned, are on my bare thighs. I shut my eyes. The temptation to peek sizzles through me, but I don't. I allow myself to experience first-hand what it's like to be dominated by a man like him.

I feel his presence behind me before he speaks. Warm breath on my ear alerts me that he's leaning in. His lips brush against the shell of my ear lightly, so much in fact that I think I've imagined it.

Deft fingertips unclasp my bra, and I allow him to rid me of the material. Once my breasts are bare, he whispers. "Put your hands behind your back, Toy." His voice is a husky rumble that shudders through me, from the top of my head, down to my toes.

I move my arms, gripping one wrist with the opposite hand. Soft rope teases my skin, causing goose bumps to dot my body. From my elbows, he binds both arms in slow measured movements all the way down to my wrists. The position juts out my breasts and curves my back.

"Open your mouth," he orders. Once my lips are parted, I feel a ball being fitted with a strap around my head. *Oh my God, a ball gag.* "Are you scared, Toy?" Without the gift of words, I shake my head, *no.*

He grips my shoulders, lifting me up onto my knees. Seconds later a cold metal object trails down my shoulder, between my heaving breasts until it reaches my belly button. Stifling a moan, I wait. Once it reaches my panties, soundlessly, it slices through the material. I know this because the breeze on my bare slick flesh has me shivering.

"You're a very good toy. Did you want to play with Daddy?" The question should freak me out. It should even make me want to stop and run away, but it has the opposite effect. I should say no, but I don't. I nod. Quickly agreeing to whatever he has in mind. "I love pretty toys, and you're exquisite." His words are filled with hungry desire. Reverence.

He trails his fingertips over my pussy and a whimper falls from my lips, which is muffled by the small ball that's positioned in my mouth. I can't stop myself from bucking against his hand. His chuckle is deep, rough, and husky. So damn sexy, I might come just by listening to him laugh.

"You're a responsive little toy. I like that. And your cunt is so wet, so damn hot. I can't imagine how good you'll feel around my big dick." He growls. And I mean, actually growls. It's the sexiest thing I've ever heard. "Do you want to feel my whip, little Toy?"

Nodding again, I wait. He shifts, I hear the shuffling of his pants, or jeans—I'm not sure what he's wearing. Then silence falls around me, covering me in its false sense of security because I know I've agreed to punishment, pleasured pain. Having no vision, makes my anticipation heighten painfully.

Moments later, the soft leather, of what I'm only guessing is a whip, trails over my ass, thighs, and calves. Lightly taunting the soles of my feet, he lifts it and with a whoosh through the air, it bites into my soles.

Another whack comes down on my calves, my thighs, and the fleshy globes of my ass. His movements are controlled, yet I can't make out their pattern. He continues his assault, again and again sending my mind into orbit.

My clit pulses with need. I want to touch myself, I want to come. To unravel and find release, but he continues whipping me. I'm whimpering behind the gag, spit drips from my lips onto my hardened nipples.

Then, he drops it without a word. I'm tugged by my arms to a standing position. "Are you still wanting to play with Daddy?" I don't have to think about it, I nod immediately. "Good girl."

His shoulder makes contact with my stomach as he lifts me over his shoulder, then sets me down onto my stinging ass. The cool wooden table below me eases the burn. With both hands on my inner thighs, he spreads me wide to his gaze.

"Your cunt is perfect. I'm going to eat you, Toy. Do you understand?" All I can do is nod. What does he think? I'm going to refuse?

His mouth crashes down onto my core, suckling, licking, lapping at me like I'm a delicate feast laid out for him. He devours my pussy as if I'm his religion and he's worshipping me. I've never had any man eat me out like this. His tongue darts between my slick folds, deeper each time he fucks me with it. His thumbs open my lips, and his growl is feral. A rabid dog eating his first meal after being starved for years.

He sucks my clit into his mouth, biting down on the hardened pink bud until I'm screaming behind the gag. "I've got myself a screamer." He chuckles as he continues his assault on me. I'm climbing up the hill into another dimension. His index finger taunts me until he strokes down my slit and finds my puckered entrance.

After my time in hell, I've never allowed anyone in there. Anal was always scary because it dredged up such dark memories, but right now as he slips one long digit into my tight entrance, his teeth graze my clit and two fingers dip into my drenched core, I don't care. All I need is release, and I find it seconds later when he violates me so fast, so deep, and so fiercely that my body spasms, and I'm coming all over his face on a loud screech of his name. At least, I think it's his name.

Fireworks, lights, and stars dot the back of my eyelids as I convulse on this man's face. My toes curl, trying to find grip on the smooth surface of the wood below me. My fingers are numb as I claw at something, anything. It's as if I'm flying and there's no gravity to bring me back down.

Moments later, as I come down from the high, I feel him slip from me, rise, and his lips brush against my ear. "Your cunt is delicious. Now you're going to learn how to swallow my dick."

THREE

ELIJAH

Her taste. Her fucking scent. I'm addicted. I want more. She's been a good girl, keeping her eyes closed as I devoured her cunt. I've never tasted anything so sweet before. Besides long ago. The girl I wanted, needed, and left. *Her.* Shaking the memory away, I focus on the woman before me. I recall the moment my finger slipped into her tight little hole between those pert ass cheeks, I made my decision, I'm claiming this toy.

Helping her off the table, I position her on the floor on her knees. The sight is arousing, erotic, and downright filthy. I make quick work of getting out of my clothes while she waits.

I've never been so hard before. My cock is steel as

I fist it. Reaching around, I undo the gag and set it on the table. "I'm going to train you to swallow my cock into your throat. Understand, Toy?" She nods. Gripping her hair, I tug her head back. "Answer me with words. I want to hear that pretty voice," I order gruffly, and she shocks the shit out of me by responding perfectly.

"Yes, Daddy," she whispers.

"Open your mouth, keep it open. I want to see you drool on my dick. Open your eyes, I want to see your beautiful eyes tear up." She flutters those lashes and her gaze pierces me painfully. Desire and hunger swirl together like a raging thunderstorm, but it's not loud, she's silent. I lean in and whisper. "Do you know why I like seeing your tears?" She shakes her head *no*. "Because I like making pretty toys cry. I enjoy breaking them."

Without further warning, I watch as her mouth opens wide and I slide straight into her throat. The tightness grips the crown of my dick, pulsing as she chokes. It's a beautiful sound, the gagging—soft gurgling, then loud retching—and all that drool.

Her big brown eyes look scared as I grip her throat and shove my cock so far down her throat, I hear the suckling sounds of her attempting to swallow. Her hands, still bound behind her back, allows her tits to jut out beautifully, catching the spit that drips from her chin. Tears stream from her eyes and I wonder how wet she is right now.

"Such a perfect pet," I whisper as I pull out, allowing her a moment to breathe. Then, I slide into her again, her mouth engulfing all nine inches. Her nose hits my lower abs again and again. Gripping her nose, I cut off her chance at breathing as I sink into her tight throat.

Once her eyes flutter, I pull out and watch her gasp. Her eyes meet mine then as she looks up at me. A messy toy. The streaks of black mascara look exquisite as it marks her cheeks.

"Are you going to fuck me now?" Her question is raspy.

I can't help smiling. She's new to this; none of my other toys would have had the audacity to ask me something like that. And as much as it would have annoyed me with any of the other girls, something about this one makes me want to teach her.

"Stand." I watch her easily rise to her feet, even

with her arms still bound behind her back. "Bend over the table." She does. Her obedience is what I've been needing, searching for. It's not forced, it's natural. I kick her feet apart and position my cock at her pussy. The heat coming off her has me aching to drive into her. Deep into a tight hole.

With my hands gripping her hips, I seat myself into her fully inch by inch. A low groan falls from my mouth, the exquisite silky feel of her cunt is like heaven. She's tight, wet, and so fucking hot. I pull out to the tip, then slam back in, knocking the breath from her lungs. Again, and again, I fuck her. I plough into her roughly.

"Oh god!" She cries out when my finger finds the tight entrance of her ass. Teasing it, I dip my finger into the vise like grip of her asshole. Finger fucking it faster, deeper, her body sucks me in, almost as if she needs me there.

"I'm going to fuck this tight hole soon," I grunt. My hips slap against her ass, making the motion of our bodies slam her into the edge of the table. Raising my hand, I slap one fleshy globe until my handprint reddens the skin. I mimic the action on the other side, marking her.

Mine.

"Please, please, please…"

Her begging only makes me harder, thicker as I stretch her cunt to fit my dick. I want to mold her to me. Make her body crave my dick like an addict needs their next fix. Reaching around, I pinch her clit hard, causing her to convulse below me as she unravels again and again. Wave after wave crashes through her, sending her into orbit, and I smirk.

Her cunt tightens around me, milking my balls of every drop of my release and I fill her unapologetically. Our breathing is labored, ragged in the dark room. My skin tingles, her body has a soft sheen of sweat and I'm tempted to taste her. To see if she's real.

Our bodies still, there's no words that need to be spoken because I'm spent. She on the other hand lies trembling on the table. I slip out of her and pull my jeans up quickly, shoving my still wet cock into the crotch.

I quickly undo the rope, allowing it to fall from her arms. Gently, I massage each limb, giving enough attention to the joints. Placing a kiss on each wrist, I regard her. Those deep brown eyes that remind me of roasted chestnuts, meet mine. They're glistening from the multiple orgasms, and her mouth lifts into a satisfied smile. Her cheeks are flushed a beautiful shade of red. Rosy. Delicate like a flower. And I wonder just how long it will take to pluck each petal until she's nothing.

"So the stories were true," she mumbles.

Quirking my head to the side, I regard her with confusion. "What stories?" I watch her slip her clothes back on. Her movements are graceful, gentle. Almost too sweet for a woman who I just savagely violated.

"I'd overheard some girls talking in the club about your penchant for choking, rope play, and a few other things," she says, her voice lowering to almost a murmur.

Shrugging, I grip her hips, tugging her against me. When I lean in, I realize I haven't kissed her yet. But before I do, I murmur, "don't believe everything you hear. If you want the real truth, you should ask the source."

Then, before she can ask, I lean in to kiss her. It's softer than I would normally take a woman, but for some reason she makes me want to show her everything. The gentle, and the rough. The dark and the light. The animal and the gentleman. My tongue dips into her mouth, hers duels for dominance, but easily gives up when I suck it hard, grazing my teeth over it in warning—I'm the Dominant, she needs to submit to me.

Her moan is swallowed by my mouth. I'm enjoying the moment, but there's a knock at the door that interrupts us, and I inwardly curse whoever the fuck is there. I pull away from her, needing space to figure out what the hell is wrong with me. I'm already craving another taste and I've only just stepped away from her.

"You better go," I say, my tone serious and commanding.

"When will—"

"I'll have you collected tomorrow night after your shift. Don't wear panties. They're the bane of my existence, I want you wet. Play with your cunt throughout the day, but don't come," I order and walk her to the door. Waiting on the other side is my driver, he nods and I plant one last kiss on her cheek before entrusting her in his care.

As soon as the door shuts, I head up the sweeping

staircase and to my bedroom. The space is a sanctuary from my dark desires. I never bring a woman in here. A toy. They're restricted to the dungeon and the makeshift living room where I have all my toys. Once the girl is comfortable, I take her down into the basement that's been set up as my own personal playroom. No woman, but Raquel has ever been in this room.

Shoving my jeans off, I make my way into the bathroom and turn on the shower. Her scent is all over me, and I'd love to revel in it, but getting attached to a toy is the mistake I made before. This time, I'm going to focus on making sure she's kept at a distance. Enough for me to fuck her into oblivion, but still retain my sanity.

The spray of the water massages the knots in my shoulders. I'm tense. I've just fucked a beautiful woman and I'm wound so tight, I'm sure I'm about to fucking snap. I want her again. I should've kept her here.

"No, you know that's a bad idea," I admonish myself as I shut my eyes and dip my head under the spray. Reaching for the shower gel, I snap the lid and squeeze out a large dollop into my hand. Rubbing it over my chest, I wash her intoxicating scent from my skin. But I know I'll never be able to rid myself of her delicious flavor. Now that I've tasted her, my lust is in overdrive, needing more. As the water sprays over me, I know in my gut that I will be returning to her for another scene. The hunger she brought about in me is raging and it needs to be satisfied.

She's so sweet, like raspberries and whipped cream. I wonder if she would give up her two jobs to work for me instead. I'll hire her as my assistant. I can have her suck me off between meetings. That will ensure I keep my sanity from the assholes we work with. I wonder if she'll accept the offer. Would she be able to work with me and be my toy at the same time?

There's only one way to find out.

FOUR

GIANA

"Hello." My voice is timid as I stare at his wife. She's slowly deteriorating, each day I come in here, I see the difference. It's worse today. Her smile is forced, she's in pain, it's written all over her face.

"I-I w-wa-anted to g-give th-this t-to you." The stuttering of her voice is more than I can handle. I've been strong coming in here, keeping her company, but now I'm finding it hard to deal with watching her die.

The envelope that's lying on the table near the bed has my name scrawled on it. "I don't think this is a good idea," I whisper the words—the same ones I tell her every day—but she ignores me as she does each time she tells me her dying wish. She attempts to shake her head, but the movement is stifled by machines, tubes, and other shit they connect to you when you're dying.

"H-he n-nee-ds you."

It's the same story. Same damn look in her eye that tells me I'm the savior of this story. If only she knew I'm the one who needs saving. I'm the one with scars on my wrist. The girl who tried to bleed out all over her parents' carpet. The one who's got something wrong with her head.

I'm an addict. I know that. My doctor explained what's wrong with me, but he doesn't know why. I haven't told anyone. It's my burden to bear. It started a long while ago, before I even turned sixteen.

"P-please?"

"I promise you, I'll be there for him." My promise is the truth. I never say something I don't mean. And I need her to close her eyes and leave this world knowing I'll do as she asked. As she begged.

I glance at her face as she once again tries to smile. I wish she'd stop. I pick up the envelope and make my way to the door. A soft croak of 'thank you' meets my ears before I leave the room with a heavy heart.

Today started out like any other day. The only difference is, I was late for work at the coffee shop. After what happened with Eli, I got home with my body still humming from the orgasms he bestowed on me. There was no explanation as to why he wanted me to leave, and I didn't ask. His driver brought me home, with another man I didn't meet following behind in my car. They made sure I was inside the apartment safely before leaving.

To say that I'm confused would be an understatement. Everything about what happened was too much, but so damn good. His mouth, his hands, and his cock. That was what set me off and I had no way of saying no. Not that I wanted to, but everything he did to me was more than I'd ever experienced.

"Hey, girl!" my best friend pipes up from behind me. Her long wavy blonde hair is tied messily on top of her head, and those big green eyes watch me with a smirk. "You look like you've been fucked." Her voice carries over the almost empty store, and I can't stop the blush from creeping onto my cheeks.

"Do you have to talk so loud?"

"That means my girl got laid. Give me all the deets!" Her excitement is palpable, but before I can even mention Eli's name, a deep gruff, yet amused tone interrupts our chat.

"The usual please, Giana."

My head snaps in his direction. Elijah Draydon looks ever the professional businessman standing at the counter with a charcoal three-piece suit and a crisp white dress shirt. His tie, a dark blue—that reminds me of blueberries—pops against the stark color of his shirt. "Yes, sir, Eli." Stumbling over my words, I grab a mug and start making the drink.

"Can you give us a moment, Leila?" He questions, caressing her name on his tongue as if he's lapping at her pussy. The thought sends jealousy swirling through me at an alarming rate.

"Yes, sure." I can tell my best friend is intrigued, but she leaves us, heading to the back of the store.

As soon as I set the mug down, his hand reaches for mine. "Giana," he murmurs seductively, making sure my panties are soaked through. "I have a proposition for you." Lifting my gaze to meet his, I hold my breath as nerves kick in attacking my belly as it flips with both excitement and anxiety.

"Is this the time and place for something like this?" My question earns me a chuckle. It's dark and seductive, just like the man himself.

"I want to offer you a job, Ms. Bianchi." The tone of his voice drops as he lifts the mug to his lips. A sensual move that has my body thrumming with need that only he can satiate.

"A job?" My brows furrow in confusion, which earns me a smirk that has my nipples hardening in the soft silk of my bra. My skin heats to a feverish level. Every movement he makes is calculated. As if he's planned it all out in his head. The scenario is his to manipulate, just the same way he controlled my body last night.

"I have an opening at the office for an assistant. Mainly taking notes, scheduling clients and court dates. The usual." He watches me like a hunter waiting to attack. The prey is caught, now all he has to do is go in for the kill. One bite and I'll be his.

Shaking my head, I take a step back. I can't do this. "Thank you, Mr. Draydon, but this… I mean I can't do that."

"Why?" he questions smoothly. "Was my cock too much for you? Or was it when you came all over my face?" His taunting queries have me blushing. Dropping my gaze, I watch his fingers tighten around the cup, and I wonder if he's worried I'll say no. That I'll do one thing that most other women won't. I'll deny him.

"I can't... I mean, working for you? How would that even work?"

"You'd dress in pretty corporate clothes, come into my office and do as I ask. Then, when I feel the need to, you'll swallow my cock and take the hot seed that spills into your pretty mouth," he tells me easily. His lips glisten from the liquid that's left behind after he's taken another sip of coffee.

The man is filthy, purely sinful, but everything he tells me has me aching, desperate for release. Lust. It drives everyone to do things they normally wouldn't. And it's pushing me closer to the edge. Elijah is dangerous. My feelings for him. The desire that seems to electrify the air around us is inexplicable. I wonder if he remembers me. If he knows at all that we've been this way before. Lovers.

"Don't forget, I'll have the driver collect you at the club at eleven. You'll stay the night so prepare yourself. I want your cunt shaven smooth because I plan on eating you till you're unable to walk." With that, he turns to leave. I watch his retreating back as it disappears through the glass doors. They shut with a click. I can't drag my eyes away from him as he makes his way to the car that's parked just outside. Before he slips into the backseat, his gaze lands on me once more. Then he's gone and I'm a mess of desire and lust. I shouldn't do it. My mind is screaming no, but my heart, pussy, and body are screaming yes, a million times yes.

"What was that about?" Leila squeaks behind me, her face the picture of confusion and excitement.

"He offered me a job," I tell her, still floating on a cloud of need for one man that has the power to make me or break me. If he knew who I was, why I was even with him in the first place, I don't think he'd forgive me.

"What?" Her chin hits the floor as she regards me, her big green eyes are wide with shock. "Tell me you accepted?"

"I… I can't…"

"Wait, why? He's rich, sexy, and he's just offered you a job where you can spend all the time in the world with him and you refused?" Leila stares at me, mouth agape in incredulity, and I don't blame her.

"I fucked him last night," I hiss, dropping my voice to a whisper.

"What?" The screech that comes from my best friend echoes through the store and has the few customers that are dotted around at the tables lifting their gazes. "Sorry!" Leila giggles, waving that everything is fine. "How did you fuck him?"

"Well, when a man and a woman—" I start but she swats me painfully on the arm.

"You know what I meant!"

"Ugh, he came into the club last night, offered me a business card and told me if I wanted to break the rules, I should be at the address on it. When I finally talked myself into going, I arrived at one of the most beautiful homes I'd ever seen," I tell her, my excitement once again returning as I recall the moment I stepped foot inside his mansion.

"Oh my God, then what happened?"

Sighing, I pick up a mug and fill it with black coffee, and before I continue, I take a long sip. "Well, he basically dominated me, ate me out…" I murmur, blushing at the memory, "and then fucked me senseless and sent me on my way."

"Shit. What's his bedroom like?"

"That's the thing, I didn't see it. We fucked in the living room, or what looked like one. I mean, it's all a messy blur." I sound like a teenage girl who's got a crush. It's stupid. I can't give him what he needs, what *she* thought I could.

"Oh, I'm sure it was, Darling. How many orgasms did he give you?"

Taking another long sip before I answer, I can't help smiling when I respond. "Three."

"And working for him would be too distracting?" she quips playfully. "I mean… I'd happily do anything he wants."

"Anything?" A deep rumble startles us both. We both turn to find the man who I know as Oliver Michaelson. His voice drips with sex as he stands at the counter with his piercing eyes on us. "Hello ladies, apparently Eli is correct, this store definitely has the best view." The man is tall, about the same height as Elijah, his hair has a dusting of salt and pepper, but is short, styled perfectly like he's just stepped off a GQ magazine advert. His face is more chiseled than Eli's. His eyes are steel, a light gray that shimmers with flecks of blue. His black tailored suit is fitted to his broad shoulders and he oozes confidence like a cologne.

"Hello, Mr. Michaelson." I smile, waiting for him to respond, instead, he pins Leila with a stare that's hungry. As if he's about to devour her in one single bite.

"You can call me Sir."

"Sir," my best friend purrs like a kitten, and I don't blame her.

"Coffee, large, black. And don't put those damn plastic lids on the cup," he orders, his eyes, alluring as they take in Leila's now trembling form. When she begins making the drink, he pins me with a stare. "And you're the new toy?" he questions, tipping his head to the side, regarding me with an inquisitive look.

"I don't know if—"

"Oh, sweet Giana, trust me when I tell you. I've known Elijah for most of his life, and when he's so wound up, it's because he's found a new toy." He leans in then as if spilling a secret. "And when I saw him stalk into the office moments ago, I knew exactly who it was, you pretty brunette." He reaches for the curl that's escaped the clip that's holding my long hair up. He twirls the lock around his deft fingers. "I trust you'll take him up on his offer. He'll make it worth your while in so many ways."

I open my mouth to respond, but can't find the words.

"Here you go, Sir," Leila says as she sets the drink on the counter.

"Thank you, Leila." He caresses her name, which has us both gasping. If I thought Eli was pure lust, Oliver is the epitome of sex. Both men are incredibly sensual and ooze masculinity. He slides a card over the counter to her. I recognize it immediately.

"That's Eli's—"

He lifts his gaze to mine and smirks. "We each have our own personalized cards. Trust me, when Eli and I want to play, we'll make sure you're both there as we devour your luscious bodies. Now, Leila." He turns to regard my friend like a feral animal. "Meet me at the address tonight at eight. Don't be late, I hate tardiness." With that he turns to leave, but halts. Glancing over his shoulder, he pins my best friend with a smirk. "And forget the panties, I don't want to waste time."

As soon as the door shuts, I turn to Leila. "You just got propositioned by one of the hottest men in this town," I tell her, folding my arms in front of my chest. She looks like she's about to burst with excitement.

"And you fucked the other one. I think it's my turn to see if his best friend can deliver as many orgasms as Eli." We're two giggling school girls at the thought of being used for pleasure by two incredibly handsome men. The only thing is, Leila doesn't know the real reason I made sure to put myself in Elijah's path. I haven't told anyone about my past. Perhaps I should. But I know deep down, it's too late for that. Too late for truths.

"I still can't work for him. It's a ridiculous offer."

"Giana, let me tell you something. A job offer is something else. More than just sleeping with him. This could be a career move, one that may result in a full-time job. And could even have you getting your dream job in a large law firm like his. I know you don't want to be in the court room, but you love solving cases. Being stuck in this shitty place for so long." She gestures at the coffee shop. "I can't let you do it. Accept the job offer, Giana. Please?"

She's right. This could be a good thing, but how can I work alongside a man I'm sleeping with? "I'll think about it. I'm seeing him tonight after work. I'm sure he'll tell me I need to decide soon."

"Listen to your head, I know your heart is saying no to the job because you could fall for him," she admits the one thing I couldn't. Only, she doesn't know I'm already in love with Elijah Draydon. I've been in love with him since I was seventeen.

"I can't think about that. You know I can't love anyone again, Lei."

"You know I didn't mean it like that, but he's a good-looking man who gets what he wants. If he wants you, I don't think you have a choice in the matter."

Once again, she's hit the nail on the head, and that's

what scares me. As much as I know I can't tell him who I really am, Elijah Draydon will be my weakness. He has been for years, seven to be exact.

I kept my distance because I was forced to. When I found myself in a predicament being left alone, an offer came along, I took it. Not knowing that it would be the biggest mistake I ever made. I submitted to a man who was no Dominant, no Master, he was an abuser.

All I wanted was Eli, but he left me. He walked out one day and I never saw him again. We made promises we both broke. But I'm done hiding. I'm done running from him. And now that I've been with him once, I don't think I'll be able to refuse or resist him again.

FIVE

ELIJAH

"I love you, I'll always love you," I whisper to her every time I walk in here. She smiles at me. She's still as beautiful as the first time I saw her. Her body is fragile, not the voluptuous curvy figure she had all the time I'd known her.

Her response doesn't come. I'm met with silence. There's no longer a woman there, merely a shell of who she was. The ache in my chest is stifling. As if someone has laid a lead weight on it, cutting off my breath.

My hand reaches for her, but she's gone. A lump forms in my throat, so thick, I'm sure I'm about to suffocate. I swallow. My lungs don't fill with air. Instead they're infused with poison. The pain of losing someone you love is a venom which slowly eats away at every cell in your body. Until there's *nothing left.*

The moment you say goodbye to the person you love, when they die, you're left alone with only the memories. The images of times you spent together are all you have, beside the things that are left behind. All those worldly possessions that now mean nothing to them.

"It's time."

My heart leaps into my throat. The tightening of my chest leaves me gasping for air. I blink to clear my vision, but it doesn't help. Everything is blurry. White coats. Doctors, nurses, they're all here to do their job. A cry, wrenched from my soul echoes from my throat and the sound surrounds me.

I'm gone.

So fucking gone and it dawns on me that I'm alone.

I'm all alone.

Shaking the memory, I glance at Oliver who's smirking at me like he's satisfied with himself. And knowing him, I can guarantee he's more than happy at what he's done.

"You did what?" I ask again in frustration.

Oliver shrugs. "I wanted to see what this toy had

that none of the other's had. To be honest, she's too innocent looking. Her friend however, I'll be testing that ride out tonight."

Scrubbing my hand over my jaw, I regard my best friend. "You're going to be fucking Leila?" He nods. "Jesus, Oliver. You can't hurt her."

"Isn't that the idea?" he wags his eyebrows.

"You know what I mean. If you break her heart…" My words trail off, but my warning is clear. He shrugs as he settles into the chair opposite my desk.

When he meets my gaze, he responds easily. "She's a big girl and I always tell them the rules before we play." With his hands poised in a steeple, his index fingers under his chin, he looks like he's ready to go to war. I wonder if he'll be able to tame the little girl.

"Good luck with that. She looks like a feisty one." And it's true. Leila, a beautiful blonde, definitely looks like she can be a handful.

"I like them feisty, that means I can tame her using punishments. There's something about the doll that makes me think she'll be up for those. My leather whip is just waiting for a perfect ass to mark." Dark eyes meet mine. Oliver is a sadistic asshole, that's why we've been best friends for more than thirty years. I first saw him when he was the new kid in the neighborhood. A ten-year-old boy who my mother told me to go and talk to. She was always on at me to make friends. I was only six at the time, but I knew a life-long friend when I saw one.

"You're an asshole, Oliver." He nods. It's no secret between us that we both have a penchant for whips and chains, but my best friend enjoys the markings, and whimpers, whereas I love the tears and hearing those beautiful sounds of choking. I've been doing this for far too long to stop now. And with Giana on the end of my cock, fingers, or tongue, I don't see any need to stop.

"As are you, man. As are you." He pushes up, rising to his full six-foot-four. "I'm heading out to meet Mr. Geizer, his assistant set up the meeting for this afternoon. I think we have a chance of signing him. Insuring the whole of Geizer Electronics will be a goldmine. Then I'm back in court to testify for that asshole Fredericks," he grunts out the name like he'd rather watch the man burn in hell. I don't blame him. Something about William Fredericks always rubbed me the wrong way. The fact that he's come to us to help him out of the insurance debacle he's been pulled into makes me wary.

"I know you can nail that bastard."

He chuckles darkly, meeting my stare. "It's his assistant I'd love to nail, but since I have a date tonight, I should be on my best behavior."

"I thought you fucked her already?" I question, watching his steel-color eyes light up with amusement. Like I said, asshole.

Shaking his head, he saunters to my office door. "Not yet, she did suck my dick once, but she's too sweet and vanilla for me." A guffaw rumbles through his chest and around my office as he steps out into the reception area that's now empty since I fired my assistant.

A quick glance at the time tells me it's almost three, which gives me enough time to get home and prepare for tonight. Picking up my land line, I dial the number for the boutique store that's my go to for my toys. "Leather and Lace, it's Kristine speaking," the sultry tone of the sales girl who knows me all too well answers.

"It's Eli here, I have a special request. I need it delivered within the next hour. Can you do that?"

"Of course, Mr. Draydon. What can I do for you?"

Once I've told her what I want, I hang up and grab my cellphone. I tap out a message with a smirk on my face. I want to have Giana screaming my name all night, and when I see her in the outfit I've chosen, there's no doubt I'll be devouring every inch of her.

There's a delivery on its way to you. Do not open the box in public. Wear it under your uniform tonight. I'll be ripping it off later. E.

I don't have to wait long for her response. It's almost immediate.

I don't need you to buy me lingerie, I do own some. And I rather like any gift I receive, so you will not be ripping anything off. G.

Chuckling, I shake my head at her feisty mouth. She's going to have to be trained properly to accept anything I buy her. And if I want to rip the fucking material off, I'll do so and she needs to learn she has no choice in the matter.

I tap *reply* and type out my response.

Your mouth will be well trained tonight, Toy. And when I tell you something will happen, have no doubt that I'll ensure it happens. With or without your consent. If I have a desire to rip, tear, or break anything, I will do so, including your beautiful body.

I wait for the three little dots, but don't see them, so I leave my phone on the desk and continue responding to important emails that have appeared in my inbox.

Once I've hit send on the last one, I check the time. Five. Shutting off my computer, I grab my keys, phone, and jacket. The reception area is silent when I step out of the office and make my way to the elevators.

As soon as the elevator arrives on our floor and slides open effortlessly and soundlessly, I step inside and push the button for the basement garage. The numbers for each floor light up as it descends. I'm delivered to my car within moments. My shiny charcoal BMW X5 sits waiting in the space allocated to it.

Pressing the key fob, I unlock the car and slide into the driver's seat. As soon as the engine purrs to life, I make my way out to the main road that will take me home.

Living outside the city has always been my goal, and when I bought the mansion in the hills, I knew it would be my favorite place to unwind. As much as I enjoy coming into town to work, and to make my weekly visits to Sins, I much prefer spending time in my own home.

As I weave out to the suburb, I can't help thinking about Giana, my sweet little toy. I'm going to enjoy tonight. Taking advantage of that incredible body has me thickening with desire already. The sun is just setting on the horizon, lighting the sky with a fiery glow.

My mind is on her while I take note of the traffic around me. Lights change. The trees that line the streets darken as the sky turns navy. The night time laced with promise of dark sins and delicious delights.

Once I arrive home, I open the gates and when they slide open, I drive up the long, paved path toward the house. Parking the car, I kill the engine, with my mind still reeling from all the thoughts of what I want to do with Giana. I should take it slow. Train her like I would any other toy, but there's something about her that tells me she's willing to do more than I gave her last night. So much more.

Heading straight for the room I fucked Giana in last night, I make sure everything is cleaned and ready. To anyone who doesn't know what I do in here, it looks like a reception room. Two large wingback chairs sit on either side of a large fireplace. There's a long wooden table where I had her kneel last night. That was a sight to behold. Her body is slim, yet her hips curve beautifully, giving her an hourglass figure.

The long brown waves that hang to the middle of her back shimmer with golden highlights. Dark eyes that stare at me inquisitively every time I walk into the room. Perfect for a toy. She needs to *feel* me as soon as I enter her space. Her awareness of me is intoxicating.

I couldn't have found a better toy. And she's all mine to train, to teach, and to consume. I'll become hers as much as she is mine. She's beautiful, innocent, yet there's a deeper need in her that calls to me.

I've spent my life after Raquel lusting after women.

None of them would ever be someone I could love, but I can deal with the desire that's one of the deadly sins. And something tells me little Giana suffers from the same.

Never have I felt such a connection to any toy. "Mr. Draydon?" Clara walks into the room carrying the shopping bags I had delivered earlier. "These arrived for you." She's worked for me for many years, since I first bought this house fifteen years ago, I had an extensive interview process to hire help around the house. I needed people I could trust. That wouldn't just walk away when they learned about what I enjoy.

"Thank you, set them down over there." I gesture at the table. "Once you're done you can leave. I'll have Lincoln drive you home," I inform her.

I've had parties here that would turn most women either green with envy, or red with anger, but Clara's turned a blind eye. She serves drinks, cleans the house, but I never allow her to see more than I would anyone else who's not into this lifestyle.

As soon as the darker side of the party takes place, she's home safe with her family. All my staff have to sign non-disclosure agreements, which keeps mine and Oliver's company running smoothly. The integrity of our business is important and he understands it as much as I do. It's our reputation which has us known as the most lucrative and meticulous insurance company in the city. We pride ourselves in offering the best rates, and the best cover to our clients. The fact that we go into court if our clients need it is one of the perks of being an exclusive client. Most of the men we do represent don't realize that if they didn't have us on their side, they'd lose millions from stupid decisions they make daily.

Once Clara leaves, the silence that settles around my home is deafening. I've never been bothered with being alone. In fact, I enjoy it, but tonight, all I want are the screams of my toy. Heading upstairs, I make my way to the east wing toward the suite I've set up for myself. None of the women I've had have ever come into this room. It's the only place that's free of the dark delights I hunger for. Even though there are many places in here where I can have a woman bound, whipped, and even bent over while I fucked her, I've never allowed myself to do it.

I promised myself that if ever I were to bring someone else here, it would be the woman I marry.Never have I set out to put a ring on anyone's finger, nobody has ever showed they're worthy. Yes, I'm an asshole, but I'm picky with women. Not everyone can hold a candle to the one I lost, and even if I do find someone that's as beautiful, broken, and sinful, it's not to say I'll walk her down the aisle.

After I lost my first wife, the only thing I could focus on is work, and fucking beautiful cunts while making them come all over me. Raquel was something else. Her statuesque frame, with flowing brown hair the color of dark chocolate. Those intense green eyes and full lips that wrapped around my cock perfectly. The moment I met her I knew I'd marry her.

When she finally said yes, and we eventually said *I do,* there was nothing that could have separated us. We were the power couple. Then, three years later, when she turned twenty-five and I was almost twenty-nine, she shied away from me. We fought all the time, and I didn't know why. Until the day we went to the doctor and he told me the truth. She was scared of letting me know she's never going to grow old with me.

She was dying and there was nothing I could do. Her choice was to hide it from me until the very end, but as she slowly got worse, there was no longer a chance for her to hide. I spent months in the hospital, each day sitting by her bedside watching her wither away into nothing. Into a shell of the strongest woman I knew.

Even as a submissive, she had a strength that forced me to my knees many a time. Nothing ever got to her. When she laid on her deathbed, begging me to move on, I still couldn't believe that she was still so damn selfless. Making sure I was happy without her, but I knew I could never be. She was my happy place, my heart and home. Now the house is a space where I degrade women, I use them and send them on their way.

She gave me a gift the day she died. A letter. I never opened it, it's still hidden in the bedside cabinet. I don't want to read her goodbyes. I wasn't ready for her to leave me. The memory haunts me to this day. It was only a year after she passed that I touched someone again. Not even a woman. A girl. The one that seemed to ensure my sanity stayed intact.

She was the first. I promised her things I shouldn't have. The same way I promised Raquel I'd care for the girl, and I broke it. That was the first promise I ever shattered and it was to my wife, on her dying breath.

I spent an intense year with Riley. A sweet, broken little blonde girl who felt the world hated her. Sadness always danced in her brown eyes, the same way desire dances in Giana's. When I first touched Riley, her body came alive. It was as if a spark had been lit inside her and she glowed. Her body trembled when I stroked her.

She was young, supple, and decadent. Seventeen and she never knew what it was like to be kissed by someone who cared for her, a boyfriend. After only a year we'd both become deeply rooted in each other. Too close. Somehow, she dragged me from the darkness and pulled my into something akin to light, almost as if I was alive again. But I didn't want to be. I lost myself in her and I felt guilty. I mourned for a year before getting into a relationship with a girl and that was what made me walk away. That was it. The intense, yet soul-satisfying romance died and I became an asshole.

Closed off, cold hearted, and filled with rage toward

a woman who isn't even alive anymore. Shaking my head, I sigh loudly into the empty bedroom. Time to get ready for my toy. Tonight will be fun breaking her in. And I intend to do just that.

SIX

GIANA

As soon as I unlock the door to my apartment, I set the box on the table and head into the kitchen. I want to open the gift Eli sent me, but I'm afraid of what I'll find inside. It's been a long day and I know tonight I'll be having an even longer session with him. After our last scene, I know he's changed from the man I once knew. He still has the sadness in his eyes sometimes. When he thinks no one is watching, I see it flicker. As soon as it appears, it's gone a second later and he pulls on the mask.

Opening the kitchen cabinet, I pull out a bottle of merlot and pour myself a large glass. Back in the living room, I pick up the cream colored box with the black logo of the store I know to be Leather & Lace. They're known for their fetish gear, and some extremely naughty toys. I've only ever been inside once. My past is dotted with the memories of implements I'd rather forget. The only fear I have now is that my old memories would bombard me the moment I begged Eli for the pain. The recollections of what *he* did stifle me. The man I trusted. I gave myself to him and he took more than I could offer, more than I ever had bargained for.

Somehow, I know Eli won't ever do that. He wouldn't hurt me, but that lingering anxiety seems to attack me from time to time. That's why it took me so long to find my way. If it wasn't for Carrick helping me, I'd never have been able to step foot inside Seven Sins. Rick trained me from day one. Molding me out of the old behaviors I was used to and into something more. Something less violent.

Lifting the lid of my gift, I unwrap the silver tissue paper and find a beautiful set of lingerie. Black bra with soft lace cups and a ruby that sits perfectly between the breasts. The straps that wrap around the chest and shoulders are made of leather. The panties are thong style, matching the bra, are leather mixed with lace. It's decadent. I've never owned lingerie like this before.

I pick up my phone and tap out a message.

Thank you for the gift. It's beautiful. G.

I don't have to wait long for his response.

It will look more beautiful on your delicious body. I can't wait to see how it fits. Don't forget, no attachments to it. Both items will be in shreds on my floor tonight. E.

Smiling, I set the phone down and take a long gulp of wine. I have a shift at the club tonight and I'm sure by the time I walk into Eli's house tonight, I'll be more than ready for him to do anything he'd like to me.

A shiver of anticipation shoots through me. My belly flip flops as I recall the orgasms he bestowed on me. The way his tongue lapped at me, delved into my core, making me scream his name. The same way he did so many years ago.

I don't have much experience with men, besides Carrick and the monster who almost broke me completely, but Eli is different. His needs border on sadist, but he gets off more on the obedience and tears. Watching a girl's desire while he takes and gives. That's one thing about him, he always gave. The only thing is, he doesn't know who I really am. He won't recognize me because I made sure that nobody can find me. I've hidden away from the man who almost killed me, but ran to the one who broke my heart. Perhaps I'm a masochist. But finding Eli again was always my dream. I wanted him, needed him more than I ever let on, and when he walked out, I forced myself not to hurt. I did though. I hurt to the very core of who I was. And maybe in my stupidity and anger, that's why I gave myself to the wrong person.

This time, I want Elijah Draydon, and nothing is going to stop me. I do want to be his toy. I know what he enjoys. I've watched him for far too long, biding my time until I knew I was ready to be owned. To be his.

It's been five long years and I'm all grown up now. Time has passed for us both, and although he's aged, he's done so very well. Still as handsome as the first day I saw him.

He tries to hide it, but I can see the agony in his golden eyes. They're the color of caramel. Grabbing my laptop, I open the lid and click on the browser. Typing in his name, I hit search and wait for the results. A few photos of him with the dark-haired woman, who was his wife for years, Raquel, at events for the company from a few years ago, pop up immediately.

Clicking on a link, I find the headline that I've read time and again over the years.

Raquel Draydon, late wife of insurance mogul, Elijah Draydon lost her battle with MS.

My heart aches for this man who's probably hurting more than anyone I've ever known. Losing myself in the article, I feel the guilt weighing heavily on me. I can't do this. My heart beats wildly in my chest at the memory of what he went through. If he ever found out about my connection, he'd never forgive me.

When I blink, the tears stream down my cheeks as my emotions get the better of me. Yes, he's an asshole, but there's an explanation as to why. He must still be so angry at the world. At losing a woman he so clearly loved. Which only seems to heighten my own pain. My own loss.

I spent two years with someone who said he cared. After Elijah left that's all I wanted. To be loved, needed, and wanted. But nothing compared to Eli. No man could come close because my young heart wouldn't allow it. I recall the memory of the day after Elijah left and I was alone in that hospital. Alone with my thoughts, those that always put me in danger.

"You're a beautiful girl," the stranger says as he walks into the room. I haven't seen him here before, but he's wearing a white coat, so he probably works here. *"I'm here to see how you're doing. Your folks said you'd had a few years struggling."* He doesn't move from the foot end of the bed, but there's something almost sinister in his gaze. Dark. Scary. Hungry.

"I'm fine."

"Now, now, I don't take well to insolent little girls. You need to respect me. Don't you want to leave here?" he questions, knowing full well I've been begging to be released. My gaze snaps to his.

"Yes."

"Will you do as I say?" The way he asks makes me shiver, but I nod. It's then that he moves closer. His hand comes out and gently strokes my cheek. It's a tender touch, one that calms me. My eyes meet his and he smiles. "Your folks said you're able to leave. That I can help you get out of here if you want to."

"Really?" He nods. For an older man, he's handsome. Dark hair with deep blue eyes. The way the curl falls down his forehead makes him look younger than he probably is.

"You're a good girl. Aren't you?" I nod. "Now, since you're going to listen to me and obey, I want you to pack your things. You're coming home with me today. I'll be able to care for you from my home."

His promise. Those words. I believe him. I push off the bed immediately, racing to the cabinet that holds the clothes and belongings that I've been allowed. Nothing sharp. No laces. Nothing that could harm me in any way. Little do they know that anything can be a weapon.

"From this moment, little one. I own you. Okay?"

I don't look at him. I can't. So, I agree without fully realizing what I'm walking into. The only thing that keeps me packing is the thought of getting out of here and finding him.

Finding the man who left me here to rot in hell.

My so-called savior was good to me for six months before the abuse started. Before my world was turned upside down. I wasn't there to heal. No. I was there to be his slave. An eighteen-year-old sex slave for a vile man.

Each time I tried to run, he found me, dragging me back to the mansion he called home. It was no home, it was an isolated dungeon filled with torturous devices, things he used to hurt me with to make himself hard.

The day I ran and made it past the gate was the day I thought I really would die. The area was so secluded I wasn't sure I'd make it very far. But I did. I stumbled into an Englishman with a heart of gold. I don't know what made me trust him. Perhaps the other girl that was in his car. Or the way he commanded attention. He offered me a phone and told me to call the police. When I refused, he did it for me.

I begged him not to send me back. I didn't want to go back to my parents who didn't want me. That's when Carrick took me in. And that's why I found Sins. I could get lost in the dark world without anyone knowing why

I was there, or who I was. My past was just that, a story that nobody knew and they didn't have to feign interest in it.

I became the girl that poured drinks and occasionally got taken up on stage and whipped, bound, and gagged. Although, there are only a handful of Dom's and Master's that I'd allow to do that to me. Carrick being one, and his partner in the club, Mason. Both men I trust with my life. But there's something about Rick that tells me there's so much he's hiding. So many secrets. Just like me.

The only person who knows about my extra-curricular activities is Lei. She never judged me. There were even a few times she came into the club, had some fun with some of the members, but for me it's an escape. A way to let go. To be free for the first time in my life.

When I first saw Elijah walk in, I was once again obsessed. I thought my eyes were playing tricks on me. But I knew it was him. I recognized him when he smiled at one of the girls. Then his gaze landed on me and my heart stopped. I waited a moment, but he never said anything. He didn't recognize me, even though I knew him.

He was dressed in a gray dress shirt, the buttons undone just enough to give me a glimpse of the smooth skin below. The dark jeans he wore hugged his thighs and ass in a way I'd never seen denim fit before. The way the dark stubble dotted his jaw, and his dark hair seemed sexily tousled. Rough around the edges, yet elegant as well, there was always something alluring about the man, but with age, he became even more so.

His dark features, and sinful smirk had me recalling everything. A young girl infatuated with a man who wasn't meant for her. Only, this time, I'll make sure he's mine.

I watched him for weeks, months, almost night after night taking women home. I'd overheard two submissives at the bar talking about him one night, about how meticulous he was. How rough he was, yet there was a gentleness to him.

That's when I knew I had to do something or I'd lose him again. I needed one night. Just one moment where I could come clean. Confess who I am. His ex-toys come in, as if addicted to him, just to get another shot at the man who's an enigma in this world, but he never gives them the time of day.

He is a drug and my addiction is at an all-time high. I need another hit. I crave another taste. I ache for another intoxicating drink. I have no doubt that only he'll be able to satiate this hunger inside me. The only problem is, if he chooses to discard me, will I be able to kick the habit, or will my past rear its ugly head and turn me into the danger I was to myself? The same one I worked so hard to abate.

Making my way into the bathroom, I step into the shower and turn on the taps until the water sprays against my fevered skin. Trying to cleanse myself of the memories of what I've endured in the past with one owner. Hoping I'll be good enough for another. For the one who holds my heart. The one I've loved since I was seventeen.

If only he knew who I was. Or why I was in his life in the first place. He wouldn't be buying me pretty panties and asking me to swallow his cock. If he knew the real scars I hide have been removed surgically. If he knew the mental wounds have been cloaked by hours upon hours of psychotherapy. Perhaps he does know.

Maybe those moments with him in the hospital were just that, his form of aiding me. Of trying to make me heal. Only... he left.

I glance at the reflection of myself through the glass shower door. As much as I hide her away, she's still there. The sick girl from all those years ago. I still see her like she's staring at me, taunting me with the ghosts of my past. All the doctors in the world couldn't change what I did. What she made me do. It's been years, I've lived with this disease. This need for someone. For affection. And as soon as people leave, I'm right back to square one. The blade on my thighs, the crimson liquid dripping from the porcelain skin.

Tears stream down my cheeks as the agony slams into my chest when the memories assault me. Gripping the wall, I cry out loudly, yet nobody can hear. My lungs struggle to pull in air. My anguish is my own. I'm responsible for my actions. Only I can change. Only I have the strength to stop, but it's difficult.

I hope he hurts me tonight. I wish he makes me cry. I want him to. The need tingles through my body as the ache between my legs starts. It always catches me unaware. Reaching between my thighs, I stroke my slick core. The smooth lips wet with arousal at what I'm going to do tonight, what I'll allow him to do to me. Shutting my eyes, I lean against the cold tiles and picture Elijah. The leather whip he wields like an expert biting into my flesh. Against my back, ass, and thighs. I want it to burn, to slice into my skin. I want him to mark me. To finally make me his like he was meant to years ago.

He promised. I need the pain. I need the pleasure. My fingers dance along my clit. Pressing the hardened nub, I beg into the spray of the water. "Please, please." My voice croaks with emotion as I cry for him. Moving my fingers faster, I dip two into my pussy. "Eli!" I cry out his name, knowing he wants it. He needs to hear what he does to me. How much I want him. My hips buck faster, needing release. My body craving it, as my digits delve deeper and faster. I'm so close. With my free hand, I reach for my neck, imagining it's his big, rough hand, squeezing. The choking sounds loud, echoing around me. Imagining his cock deep down my throat. I gag. I want the saliva to drip onto my breasts.

I picture it perfectly. Being his toy. Only his.

He bids me to come for him. To find release only for him. He's mine as I am his. And I do. Pinching my clit hard, my body convulses wildly as I once again scream his name until my voice is croaky, and my throat burns.

When I come down from the high of my orgasm, I open my eyes and find the water running cold and my face flushed. Shutting off the water, I step out of the shower and wrap a towel around me. My legs are still wobbly, but my face is the picture of innocence.

The face of an angel and the heart of a devil.

That's what my uncle used to say when I turned thirteen. When he first started noticing I wasn't his little girl anymore. The day he knew I wasn't the innocent niece he'd loved all my life. I turned into something else. Only, he didn't know why. I was unruly. A bitch is what he called me one day. He told me little whores were meant to be broken. So that's what he did, he broke me. My virginity he could never steal, but it was what he did when he took my ass and made sure I didn't sit down for a week. It was then I knew I'd never be the same again.

Over time, I'd hungered for the pain to forget what had been done to me, it was only when Elijah touched me the first time I realized sex could be more. It could be different. Then, once again after I escaped my tormentor my desires had changed. Carrick taught me, molded me into something new. A shiny penny from a dirty dime.

As soon as I looked up at Elijah, I called him Daddy, not because of my past, but because I knew the kind of Dominant he is. I overheard things about him. His penchant for being the older male, and it makes me wonder if he's still thinking about me when he fucks them. When I called Eli Daddy when he fucked me, I came harder than I ever did in my life. My sick mind can't differentiate between a normal relationship and a dark, sadistic one.

I know I'll never be a normal girl.

It's not how I've been made, how I've been programmed. When I lost my virginity to Keegan Jeffries in the boys' locker room at the age of thirteen, I knew then and there that I wasn't like the other girls in school, but I didn't care. The wrong that I did was what gave me the rush. The high of doing something I shouldn't be doing.

Maybe that's why I turned into the nut job everyone

wanted locked up. Maybe it was the day I sucked off my math teacher, or the night I fucked three boys from our football team. Perhaps the day my stepbrother decided I was the girl he wanted to test choking on his cock. Little did he know I was far more experienced than he thought. He couldn't hurt me. He did try though. He gave it his best shot.

Pulling the panties Elijah bought me up my slender legs, I take a look at the fit in the mirror. Perfect. Once I've clasped the bra in place, I can't help smiling. It's stunning. Quickly, I dress in the uniform we're meant to wear and pull my wet hair into a clip, allowing a few strands to hang down, framing my heart shaped face. Keeping my make-up light, I dab gloss on my lips, leaving them shiny.

Once I have my purse, keys, and phone in hand, I make my way out the door. *I'm coming for you Mr. Draydon. And I can't wait.* My body is already thrumming with anticipation. At the thought of his touch, my clit tingles. I'll drench these panties just like he wanted. I want to please him. It's as if it's woven into my being.

Slipping into the driver's seat of my car, I put my

foot on the gas and head over to Seven Sins for my shift behind the bar. I'll be counting down the hours until closing time and that's put a smile on my face as I make my way to work.

SEVEN

ELIJAH

The doorbell dings through the house and I know it's her. Anticipation courses through me like a white-hot pain that sizzles in my veins. My blood heats, tingling through every inch of my body, causing my cock to throb.

The agony of need. The hunger of lust.

I've never been filled with this much eagerness when a new toy arrives. When I reach the door, I still for a moment, inhaling a deep breath, and then pull it open. The heavy wood slides open and I'm met with the beautiful brown eyes of Giana. "Toy," I murmur, leaning in to press a soft kiss to her cheek. There's a sizzle of desire that shoots through us at the connection.

"Eli." My name on her lips is an aphrodisiac, it turns me into a beast that would love to devour her right here on the doorstep. Stepping back, I allow her to enter. I reach for her coat. As soon as she sheds the offending item, I'm met with her smooth skin and long flowing hair, which covers what I want and need, her bare skin. Her tank top offers me glimpses that causes my hunger to skyrocket.

"I trust you had a good night at work?" I question as I lead her indoors. The room I fucked her in last night is lit with candles giving it an ethereal glow. I watch her shrug at my question, the movement causing the soft fragrance of her skin to drift my way. A scent of sweetness and innocence. A flower, perhaps a bright red rose, both beautiful and alluring, the color of lust. I wonder if I'll be the one to crush her or make sure she blooms. I watch her for a moment longer and I see it. My flower. Unopened, waiting for me to walk in and pluck her.

"It was busy. There was…" She blushes when she meets my gaze. "There was a show." Her deep chocolate gaze darts around nervously. A soft blush on her cheeks tells me she's utterly embarrassed by something and I'm dying to know more.

"Tell me, sweet toy." I reach up, stroking her cheek. "Look at me." She lifts her stare to meet mine. "Never be scared to tell me anything. This agreement we're entering into, it's important that you are honest, brutally honest."

"There was something I saw, I've just…" Her cheeks darken to a dark red rose color. "I wanted to try it, but fear got the better of me, so…"

"So… you wanted to know if I could do whatever it was to you?" She nods slowly, almost too innocently, and I have a feeling I'm going to enjoy whatever it is. Her lips, full and plump, curl into a smile that's both seductive and mischievous. "And what exactly did they do?"

"He… the Dom, whipped her, took her into subspace where she was crying from pleasure. It was pure. It was emotional. There was such a rawness to it, that…"

Before she can voice the rest of her sentence, I reach for her cunt, cupping it in my hand. Her heat is scorching. I'd love to take her there. To make her feel everything she's talking about. It's something a Dominant and submissive can achieve, but it needs to have full trust. When pain becomes so intense, the senses are heightened in such a way, it's almost as if the sub is floating in her mind.

"Did you come?" I ask, allowing one finger to stroke the seam of her body. Shaking her head, she covers my hand with hers, pressing our combined touch to her core.

"I… I did," she confesses. It's then her darkened gaze flits up to meet mine in a ferocious standoff. The lust that shines and burns in her eyes is something I've never seen in any woman. Not even Raquel. "Will you show me? Can you take me there?"

It's not a question, she's pleading, begging for it. Many submissives beg for orgasm, or more spanks, anything, but something in the way Giana is practically salivating at the thought, turns my restraint from one hundred to zero in the blink of an eye.

"You disobeyed me?" I question, still with my fingers on her mound. She nods slowly, knowing that she's in for a punishment. But, before we get there, I want her to eat, she needs her strength. "Why do you want to go there, Toy?" Something shifts between us then. I don't know if it's her need or my craving, but the air is heavy with an unspoken truth. We're both broken souls. Both searching for more out of the cards we've been dealt, but not finding it apart. It's been a couple of days, not long at all, but she's given me what I needed.

"To forget, to be free," she says, and I know it's the truth.

Nodding, I smile. "I'll do it, but not tonight. First, we'll eat and then we'll play. I want to learn about you, Gia. Everything there is to know."

Last night, her body relented. Bowing to my needs the way I want my submissive to be, she allowed me in. And I want to delve deeper. I need to know what makes her tick. I want to learn all there is to know about this sultry goddess.

"I take it you're on the pill? If not, I suggest we get you on one immediately. I hate condoms," I say gruffly.

"I am, have been for many years," her words are whispered. Soft and sweet.

When I first laid my eyes on Giana in Sins that night, I knew I'd have her. There was an innate perverseness in the way she'd stare at the shows on stage every night. As if it was her way of finding herself. Her need and her truth. We all go to Sins for different reasons. I find women who want that Daddy Dom kink. They need the pleasure and pain and want it from an older man. I give that and more. The only thing I've never done was take a long-term sub. Never kept one or wanted to own one.

"Come," I say, pulling my hand from her body and guiding her to the table that's been set with our dinner. Two plates, one glass of wine to calm her down, and water for me. Once we're seated, I watch her before speaking once more. "Tell me, Giana. Why exactly do you need to go there?" I need the truth.

She lifts her gaze, pushing my middle finger into the material of her soaked thong, and I almost come from the slick juices that soak it. Then, she moans her confession. "I want freedom from the memories."

I'm not sure what she means. I search her eyes; they've darkened to an endless black abyss of confusion, fear, and yearning. "If pain is all you'll need to be free, sweet Toy. I'll gladly take you there, but you need to trust me implicitly."

"I do," she affirms boldly.

Her confidence is intoxicating. Confusion is at the forefront of my mind as to how this beautiful woman can be so broken. But more so, I wonder how she can give me, a man she's only known for a short time, all her trust. It normally takes months, years to get to a point of such openness and trust for any relationship. Especially when she's asking me to take her to a place of utter and complete unawareness. Where she will need me to care for her, because when she reaches subspace, she won't be thinking clearly. It's as dangerous as much as it is beautiful and freeing.

"Who hurt you?" I demand. My tone is no nonsense, an order rather than a question.

I'm expecting an honest answer from her, but her eyes give her away immediately, and the lie that slips from her mouth has anger barreling through me. "Nobody." When she stands and turns away from me, I follow. Gripping her shoulders, I tug her back against my solid chest. Leaning in, I rest my chin on her shoulder and my hands on her arms, holding her steady.

"Listen, little Toy. Never. Ever. Fucking lie to me.

Understood?" A violent shudder travels through her frame, and I can't help smiling. A little fear instilled in my toys always makes me happy. It's part of what gets me off. Why I enjoy this life.

"I didn't lie. I just didn't give you the answer you wanted. Nobody hurt me. I did it to myself."

The truth slips from her, and I know with all I am that she's giving me what I asked for. She's offering me her, all of her. She turns in my arms, her face tipped up to mine. Raw honesty shines in those dark eyes. I want to make everything right; I want to fix her.

Who the fuck are you kidding? You can't even fix yourself.

"Cocky toys get punished," I warn.

"Then punish me," she whimpers, the words dripping with desire. Her eyes dance with the challenge and I smirk with satisfaction.

Gripping her wrist, I drag her to the back of the room. The wooden bench that sits waiting for us is exactly where I want her. The view of the garden sits beyond, lit up with soft candles. She wouldn't be able to see further than the patio, but it's enough to give her something to focus on while I make her pay for being a cheeky toy.

She wants to be punished? She'll be punished. Without a thought, I tug the zipper of her dress until the material pools at her feet. The lingerie I bought looks exquisite on her beautiful body. Every curve, each incredible inch, has my mouth watering. I want to make sure all she offers me tonight is her complete and utter submission.

I don't know why. I can't explain it. But I want all of her. Every damn inch. All her moans, whimpers, and pleas. They're all mine. I will own them. No other man will give her what I can, and will. For the first time in a long while, I'm alive.

"Too bad I won't enjoy this scrap of material," I growl, gripping the leather straps that lie over her shoulders and hug her beautiful breasts. I pull the small blade from my pocket and slice through each strap. Once the bra is at her feet, I spin her to face me. "Sit on the bench. Don't move." The order is clear. She obeys without refusal, settling herself on the wood. I grab the rope and kneel at her feet. Gently, I twine the thick silk rope around each ankle, leaving enough for her wrists.

"Lie back."

Once again, she submits to my demand and reclines on the long-cushioned bench. Since it's shaped like an upside-down T it will have her at my mercy. I grab her left ankle, making sure she's bound to the wooden leg, then fasten the rest of the rope to her left wrist. Mimicking the action on the right side of her body, I stand back and regard her spread legs. Open to me. For me to taunt and tease. For me to devour as I please.

"You look utterly delicious, Toy," I tell her. Watching those eyes glisten, I can't help grinning when she opens her mouth to respond, but she's left speechless.

I reach for the thin flogger that's lying beside the bench and lift it, making sure she sees exactly what I have in hand. When I raise the slim leather toy and bring it down on either thigh, she whimpers, tugging on her restraints, but I know she's bound perfectly. *You're not getting away this time, Toy. Or ever again.* My mind confirms. I'm keeping her. She's mine.

I continue my assault on her body. On her smooth, creamy flesh. She's stunning, lying there bound for me. Needy and wet, but begging for mercy. The small red prints on her creamy flesh make me thicken in my slacks. "What—" Before she can voice her concern, I spank her again and again. Small red markings appear on her creamy skin, my initials E. D. which are engraved on the flogger, prominent on the porcelain flesh.

"You're not allowed words, Toy. Remember you're playing my game now." Lifting the leather, I bring it down on her pussy, which is covered by the lace material, earning me a loud *thwack* and her loud cry.

I watch the tears form in her eyes; they glisten like black diamonds in the candlelight. I find myself entranced. Like never before. *What is this toy doing to me? Why do I lose all control with her?*

"Please, I… I need…"

"You need to come? You've already come, without my permission," I taunt. "Didn't you?" She nods. Picking up the knife, I hold it up to the light, causing it to glisten. Her eyes widen; she watches me in awe. There's no fear in her expression. Merely excitement, desire, and shock. I lean in, watching her chest rise and fall with quick breaths. I trail the sleek silver blade over her nipples, each one hardened to little pebbles.

I'm tempted to taunt them, bite them and suck them into my mouth. But for now, I refrain. "You have beautiful tits, Giana." My use of her name instead of *Toy* startles me, as well as her from the look on her face. She is mine to play with, yes, but as I watch her writhe under the soft leather, something inside me shifts. Emotion. Need. It's fierce, unyielding, and I know she can feel it too.

I slowly edge the blade down her body, teasing it to her bellybutton, I hook it into the diamond ring that's pierced through her flesh. A slight tug has her whimpering, and my dick fighting its way from my slacks.

Watching with rapt attention as she licks her lips, her gaze pinned on my movements. I won't hurt her, but she doesn't know that. This is a test of her trust in me. I have to make sure she's giving me everything. Submitting fully. She lifts her gaze then, her head resting on the wood, and she smiles.

"Please…" Her voice is raspy, filled with longing.

"Begging isn't going to make this go any faster, but I do enjoy hearing it." I smirk, running the tip of the blade over her cunt. An unmistakable tremble travels over her when I press down on her clit. The material hinders any further movement, but she sucks in an audible breath.

I move my hand, along with the silver blade to the waistband of the panties, and slice them from her hips. As soon as they fall, she's bare to my gaze, just how I want her all the time.

"Your cunt is perfect." My murmur is filled with reverence as I take in the smooth flesh, glistening and intoxicating. Kneeling at the bench, my face is in line with the drenched pink entrance of her body. "You're so wet, Toy. So responsive to the pain." Lifting my hand, I tease her slit with the cold steel, and another gasp of shock falls from her plump lips. "Do you like the anticipation, Giana? The fear that's coursing through your veins as I tease your cunt with the knife?" My tone is raspy with desire. My cock is so hard it could break through the fucking wood right now. If I fuck her in this instant, I won't last long.

Rising, I tug off the T-shirt I'm wearing and drop it to the floor. Her eyes are wide as she drinks in my body with her heated gaze. It both warms me and scorches me at the same time with a single look.

"Please, Eli. I need it," she rasps with such innate longing that it tugs at my chest.

Her pleading sounds erotic, sensual. A soft whimper that makes me want to punish her some more just to hear it. The begging is something that I normally hinder by fucking their throats, but with her, I crave it.

I don't respond. Instead, I lift the crop, with a small leather tip, and bring it down on her clit. Harder and harder. Her cries are fuel; they're lightning strikes to my skin and they burn and sizzle through me. Heating my blood with a desire so ferocious I could burn down the whole goddamn house.

"Do you want my cock, Toy?" I grunt. Her head moves quickly, nodding. With her open like this, I could take either hole. I'm aching to drive into her tight ass, to feel it squeeze me, sucking me into her body.

I continue my assault. Her beautiful pussy is turning a deeper shade of red, and I lick my lips at the stunning sight of it. Her thighs are trembling as she tugs on the restraints. She's close to orgasm, I can tell by how her moans and breathing change. Her chest rises and falls quickly as she tries to calm herself.

"Do not come," I warn. Immediately, I stop spanking her clit, leaving her convulsing on the bench, her arms tugging on the tether. I can't wait anymore. Everything about her turns my lust into a raging inferno. Unbuckling my belt, I tug it from the loops, and drop it with a loud thud on the floor. My slacks and boxers find themselves in a heap of material and I step up to her. Gripping my cock in my fist, I tease her wet cunt with the crown, painting her with my pre-cum. Marking her.

"Fuck, please, please, please!" she cries out. The agony lacing her tone is more than I can bear, so I drive into her, seating myself fully inside her body in one long thrust.

"This what you wanted?" I pull out and slam back in. Again, and again, my body plunges, thrusts, and violates her beautiful tight hole. I know she's close when I feel the flutter of her inner walls around my shaft. Slick with arousal, they coat my erection.

My hips slam into her. The table squeaks on the floor. This is violence, this is raw unadulterated fucking. There's no love here. I can't allow that emotion to infiltrate what I do. But when she lifts her head, there's something shining in those pretty eyes.

She regards me with a look that tells me I'm saving her.

From what? I don't know.

All I do recognize is the thankfulness, the joy, and the pleasure I'm giving her.

Reaching for her clit, I tug and twist it until she's screaming. Her eyes roll back in her head and her legs tremble; her hands tug at the restraints.

"Fuck! Eli!" Her voice is raspy.

Her throat must be aching by now. With my free hand, I lean in and grip her throat. Teasing her clit, taking away her breath, I fuck her relentlessly until I feel it. Her walls tighten, they grip me in a vise hold, squeezing me.

"Milk my fucking dick, Toy. Take all my seed." My grunts are feral, growled like a fucking beast. Basal desire, animalistic need, and filthy hunger drive us into oblivion as I mark her from the inside as she marks me. Our release shatters us both, and I wonder in that moment if our broken pieces will ever be mended again.

EIGHT

GIANA

Once the ropes fall away, Eli massages my limbs gently. His touch is vastly different to the way he just fucked me. As if he's now closed off the side of him that's volatile, the anger and rage hidden behind the gentleman that's caring for me. I've never felt such an intensity as I do with him.

"Are you okay?" he questions in a low, calm tone. Caramel eyes meet mine, causing me to smile. Emotion is evident in his gaze. It warms me, as if he's trying to hold me with a single glance. Keeping me safe from all I fear.

"Yes." My own response is whispered as he helps me off the bench. A wobble in my knees makes him wrap his arms around my waist, tugging me against his warm skin. Lifting my gaze, I meet his. There's a tenderness in his expression that steals my breath. The way he's looking at me is not the way I expected him to. There's too many emotions swirling around us, and even though I've known him for half my life, he doesn't know me. At least, he doesn't recognize me. I'm no longer a girl. I'm grown. A woman. A toy.

"This… I don't…" he starts, but shakes his head. Lifting me easily in his strong arms, he sets me down on a plush leather sofa. The man is torn, I see it in the depths of his shimmering eyes. He's warring with himself and I'm not sure how I can fix him. Or even if I want to. I like the broken man. His pieces fit with mine. It's always been like that. I want to tell him. In this moment, right here, I think about confessing who I am. But when he turns his back to me, I feel it, that niggling in my gut. Fear. Anxiety. They grip me. Gnawing at my insecurities, at my addiction for him. This isn't love. I'm stupid to think it is.

All we had was lust.

Voracious. Hungry. Dangerous.

The problem is, I fell. A long time ago. I fell in love with the man before me. And now I want more. I need more. "Eli—"

"I'm wrong for you on so many fucking levels, Giana. The darkness inside me, it's… I want to hurt you. I want to make you cry." He pivots on his heel, pinning me with a glare. "I want to fucking break you." The words are hissed in a feral growl. But it's when he drops to his knees before me, gripping my thighs as if I'm the one who can save him, that I realize he wants me more than I bargained for. I thought I would have to play a game with him. To *make* him want me. But I don't. He holds onto me, his fingers pressing painfully into my flesh.

"I'm already broken, Elijah. Can you not see my fragments? They're in your hands. Just look closer. See me," I plead, the words unbidden, yet true, falling from my lips. I want him to see the girl he left. The one that gave him her heart and body. Our gazes are locked in a standoff. There's no going back. I can never take back what I've just said.

He stares at me for such a long time, I wonder if he's

ever going to respond. I hold my breath, hoping for a miracle. Praying to a god that never gave me anything, that I don't believe in, to just this once, show me this is real. "Who hurt you?" he asks again. The question he voiced earlier brings the bile from my stomach up to my throat, burning with the truths I want to tell him, but I don't. Instead, I push his hands from my legs and stand.

I wish he wouldn't ask me questions that I can't give him the answers to. If he knew, there'd be no way he would keep me. I want him to keep me. To own me.

"Giana, you can trust me. I need to know what you're hiding."

"I don't trust anyone, Eli. It's nothing personal, but my life, my past, isn't something I like to talk about. All you need to know is that I'm here, if you want me."

His hand on my shoulder stills me, and the warmth of his breath fans over my cheek. "Look at me," he orders.

Turning to face him, I try to lift my gaze. My lips quirk into a wry smile, one to offer some indication that I do trust him, but I can't give him more than I am right now.

"I want you. Be mine. Let me own both your mind

and your body. I'm not asking for your heart because I can't give you mine. When you walk in here, you'll be my toy. But there is one cardinal rule I have that you cannot break."

The earnestness in his voice is enough to have my heart stuttering. It wants to leap into his hands and beg for ownership, but like he said, it's not what he wants.

Need overrides my fears. "What is the rule?" I ask.

"Never lie to me, you need to tell me the truth. Everything. Or I will find out on my own."

The demand in his words are clear. If I don't tell him, he will use his own sources to find out why I'm so fucked up. Why my life took the turn it did. And he'll also find out who I really am. What I've been through with William, the man who owned me, is something I'd rather not have anyone find out. The vile things, the disgusting agony I endured with him, is something I want buried. Only, I know that secrets don't stay six-feet under for long. Skeletons always escape their closets that we hide them in.

I was forced into the life I led for so long. Made to hurt. Made to crave the pain and the chaos that turned me into the addict I am. The pain he bestows on me makes me ill and it turns me on. My mind is warped, convincing me that sex is bad, but it feels good. Being spanked, whipped, and caned makes me wet and turns me on. Although, right now, there's only one man who can do that to me, and he's standing before me waiting for me to give him an answer. Shaking my head, I turn away once again. I can't meet his inquisitive stare right now.

"Giana—"

"No, I can't tell you right now. I need time." I can't believe I'm thinking of telling him the truth. About telling him what happened to me the day after he walked out. The day he left me there, in that hell. How my mind is shattered into a million pieces and I have no control of my actions. Since being owned by a monster, I've found a way to hide the urge to hurt myself and that's how my love of pain has made me who I am today. I have control.

He tugs me from the sofa, pulling me over to the wall opposite the wooden table where he had me bound and helpless only moments ago. "Bend over and hold the railing." His raspy, gruff command drips anger, frustration, and desire. The silver pole that adorns the cabinet before me beckons with a shiny glint. I reach for it, bending at the waist. I'm too aware that we're both still naked. We're both still trembling with need. The air is thick with yearning and lust. It's heavy, like a weight hanging over us, making sure we're slaves to it.

"What are you doing?" My question goes unanswered and the anticipation that sizzles through me is enough to have my legs weakening. I'm in for a punishment, I don't know what it is, but god knows I need it. My clit throbs, my pussy is soaked with a mixture of our release, and my inner thighs are sticky with Eli's cum staining my flesh.

"You are going to answer me. With each unanswered question, I'll whip you. This cane," he murmurs as he trails the thin wooden stick over my bare ass, "is going to lick your skin the way I would. Only, it's going to hurt a hell of a lot more." Without warning, he brings the bite of pain down on my flesh, which has me raising up onto my toes and yelping into the candlelit room.

"Eli—"

"Tell me who hurt you, Giana," he orders. With

another swat on my ass, I bite down on my lower lip so hard I draw blood. The metallic taste is enough to have the memories flooding back. Images slam into me; behind my shut eyes, I see clearly. Each sordid picture is pure agony. More so than the wooden cane burning into my ass each time he whips me.

"I can't."

"Toy, you are to obey me," he grunts angrily.

There's no choice in the answer because if I don't tell him, I'd be breaking a rule. An unspoken one, but one nonetheless. I hear the whoosh in the air of the cane. I feel the sting again and again.

I lose count of how many times he brings it down onto the cheeks of my ass. The burn, the beautiful sting, is intense. And my brain, my exquisitely sick mind, revels in it. My pussy aches, throbs, and pulses. I'm soaked from the smarting.

I think it was twenty when he bites out through clenched teeth. "I'm not going to—"

I don't let him finish as the confession falls from my lips. "My uncle!" I cry out. I let out the acknowledgment that I'm tainted. I'm not the sweet girl everyone thinks

I am. The tears that I was holding onto for so long spill. Dropping my voice to a mere whisper, I repeat the words I never told anyone. Not the doctors, not my parents, and not even my best friend.

The harsh echo of the wood dropping to the floor surrounds me. But it's not that sound that allows me solace, it's when Eli thrusts his hard cock into my pussy so deep I feel him in my stomach. "Your cunt is mine. Do you hear me, Giana? Every fucking inch of your body is now mine. I'm going to fuck all those memories from you. I'm going to take your mind and salvage what I can, and then I'm going to rebuild you into something more."

His vow is more than I can handle. My sobs are loud, echoing around us. As the emotions drip steadily down my cheeks, I remember the moment I became *different* to my friends. The memory expunges itself from me. I was no longer innocent. I was a broken girl, worthless and tainted. The fat tears also allow the pain from the Master who tortured me to dissipate in that moment. It's not the pain of his whip or cane, but of my past that relinquishes me of my sick history.

I want Eli to save me. I need him to give me more, and he does. His body slams mine against the cabinet. His hands are gripping my hips painfully. Strong fingers bite into the flesh, pinning me in place. We're no longer two people, but one as our bodies fit together like they were meant to.

The sounds of sex—slapping skin, grunts, and moans—swirl in the room, surrounding us in pleasure. And as Eli ploughs into me, I let go of everything. Sadness and relief runs in salty tears down my cheeks. He grips my hair, tugs me back against his chest and my lips find his. The kiss is brutal, it's all consuming, he's stealing every breath and giving me his instead. We're one. Connected. Molded into one sweaty being, made of lust and desire. Of darkness and the filth of my past. His cock hits a spot inside me, and I see stars.

"Come for me, Toy. Come on my dick because I fucking own you now."

And I do. My body obeys him and my mind… it's convinced. This man will be my undoing. And I'll be his.

NINE

ELIJAH

Gulping the harsh alcohol, I watch the stars twinkle in the dark sky. I put her to bed after I fucked her harshly, bent over taking my cane, like she was born to do it. This girl has fractured the walls I built. I don't know how to care for someone. If I allow her in, I'll never get her out.

I'm having a drink on the terrace, watching the lights flicker in the distance with my mind on two women. My wife who's probably watching me from heaven wondering what the fuck is going on. And the other is the woman who's asleep in a bed I'd set her in. The first of my Toys to ever see more of my house than the playroom.

The night air is cool, but it does nothing to quell the

blood that races through my veins. She's everything I ever needed in a woman, but before I can even consider more, I need to know what happened to her. Why she's so fucking broken. Every time I look in her eyes it's as if a small piece of her is begging for me to save her. For me to be her knight in shining armor, but I don't know if I can.

Will my own needs not make her worse? I'm tempted to find her uncle and make him pay for whatever he did to her. To make him suffer. "It's cold out here," her soft voice, tentative and innocent, filters through the thoughts of murder that swirl through my mind.

"You should be sleeping," I tell her, but I don't look behind me. I don't need to. Her body heat nears, and it's as if we're two opposite ends of a magnet, I sense her. My body longs to connect with hers.

"I was. When I woke up you weren't there," she murmurs.

I want to touch her, but my chest aches. Since I lost Raquel, then walked away from Riley, this is the first time I've allowed someone to get under my skin like this, but only because I know her secret. I thought I'd given up on affection. On emotion. But somehow, Giana has convoluted my whole world.

"I don't sleep beside my toys," I bite out. I'm not angry at her, I'm frustrated at myself. A soft gasp from her is the only way I know my words have hurt her. They slice through the sensitive woman that hides behind the walls she's built over the years. Her pain is mine. I feel it in my chest. "If you want to go—"

"I'd like you to come lie with me," she interrupts.

I should hold her. I'm turning into a cold-hearted bastard and that's the last thing I want to do with a woman like her. Someone so shattered by life. Turning, I face her fully. She's dressed in my white dress shirt I wore earlier. The hemline sits just below her ass and pussy. Buttoned up just enough to tease me with her full tits, she's rolled up the sleeves, which gives her an innocence she no longer possesses.

Her hair is messy and her big eyes peek up at me from under dark lashes. Her lips are full and plump, begging me to taste them once more. To own them. *How did I ever become such a mess?* I think to myself, wondering where I went wrong.

"Like I said—"

"If you want to know who I really am," she says, stepping closer, her hand resting on my shoulder, causing the skin to sizzle with need for her. "Then you'll allow me the pleasure of your company."

When she's obeying my every whim, she's beautiful. When she's screaming out my name and crying with tears of pleasure, she's intoxicating. But it's when she's confident in her own skin, that's when she becomes my addiction. My lust. My Toy.

Closing the distance between us, I wrap my arms around her. My hands roam gently over her curves, finding purchase on her pert little ass. I lift her up. A small wince on her face tells me she's still tender from earlier.

"I'm sorry if I hurt you." My words are a shock to me. I still for a moment as realization settles that I'm showing her affection. Giving her a part of me I've kept hidden for so long it feels foreign. I've never apologized to any of my toys before. Never needed or wanted to.

"You didn't." Her legs wrap around my waist, her arms circle my neck, and her face is only inches from mine. Her eyes shine in the moonlight. A beacon in the darkness. "I wanted you to make me forget. There's so much wrong with me, I don't know why you'd want me."

"You make me want to do things to you I've never done with anyone else." My confession makes her smile. "What?" I question, still holding her against me, her ass cheeks in my hands. Her tits against my bare chest, and her mouth inches from mine.

"You have no idea how much I want you." She rolls her hips, causing me to groan as the heat of her pussy presses against my crotch.

"Oh, Toy, I do. Every fiber of my being knows because I don't just want you, I need you. I should push you away," I murmur while dropping my gaze, needing to clear my mind of what she does to me. Looking into her eyes is hypnotic, I find myself saying stupid things. Words I shouldn't be telling her.

"But you can't," she utters.

The truth of her words delves into my heart and mind. She's right. I can't deny it. Each night I walked into Sins, I saw her, wanted her, but never took the opportunity to ask her. This wasn't by chance, I've wanted her for a long while now. Snapping my gaze to meet hers, I'm astounded by the strength that shines in hers.

I walk us into the house once more. Still holding onto her, I pad up the staircase and down the hall. I take her to the guestroom I settled her in earlier after our scene. A beautiful queen size bed sits against one wall with the walk-in closet opposite, and an adjacent dresser. The windows overlook the countryside, which is at the rear of the house. Cream and peach colors adorn the walls, giving it a feminine feel.

I set her down, my hands missing her warmth as soon as she steps away from me. She glances around as if seeing the space for the first time. I'm sure she didn't notice anything when she awoke.

"It's pretty," she murmurs, running her hand over the delicate fabric of the curtain. Her fingertips gently tug them open only to be met with the dark window beyond.

"You're pretty."

She pivots on her bare feet to stare at me. The corner

of her gentle mouth tugs into a playful grin. "I'm no prettier than the other toys you bring here."

The fact that she's seen me with other women, yet says it so nonchalantly, makes me wonder if it bothers her. Perhaps she's jealous. I want her to be. Not because I'm an asshole, but because it shows she cares. That she's feeling what I am.

In that moment, I wish I can remove my past. Erase all the women who've been on the end of my dick. So many nights I've enjoyed devouring sweet, beautiful toys, but with her, there's nothing I want more than to take her to my bedroom and watch her sleep tangled in my sheets. To have her scent in the room I think of as my sanctuary.

"And what do you know of the others?"

She turns away from me again. I hate that. The need to have her eyes on me all the time tugs at my chest. "I know they enjoyed being with you. That they come into the club to see you in the hope that you'll take them for a second time perhaps. That you'll gift them the title most of the women who frequent Sins covet."

Chuckling, I scrub my hand over my jaw as I regard

her still dressed in my shirt. "And what title is that, Giana?"

She glances at me over her shoulder. The sight knocks me breathless. Her big brown eyes pierce me, the long chocolate waves of her hair fall in an alluring waterfall down her back. The shirt teases a hint of her ass cheeks, and the way her lips purse tells me there's something devious on her mind.

"Daddy's Toy," she breathes, like a seductress tempting a man who has no control.

And I don't. Every restraint I was holding onto snaps in that moment, and I'm overcome with an insatiable need to claim her. To make her my toy forever.

Stalking toward her, I near her within a few steps. The sweetness of her perfume invades my senses when I lean in. Brushing my lips over her cheek, I revel in the shudder that ripples through her. "I'd like you to tell me something, Giana. Is that what you want? The coveted title of Daddy's Toy?" I ask, barely grazing her lips with mine. The words fan over her face. Her eyes flutter closed, those deep breaths she was inhaling are a thing of her past when I reach for her face, cupping it in my hand. My thumb strokes her cheek, the smooth skin feels like silk under my touch. She leans into me, and I recognize her need is as palpable as mine. A force living and breathing between us. "Tell me, Giana."

"Yes," she whimpers.

A keening cry falls from her lips when I grip the hair at the nape of her neck, tugging it back so her face is in line with mine. I'm not letting her go, she better believe that when she agrees to this, I'm keeping her. "Open your eyes." My command is gruff, heavily doused in desire. When those endless dark pools open and meet mine, I see it. Lust. "Do you want to be my Toy? Do you know what that means, Giana?"

She attempts to shake her head *no*, but my grip on her hair is too tight. I want words. She knows this. "Tell me, Elijah. Explain to me, let me hear you."

"It means you give over control to me. Which means I own every aspect of your life. You're allowed to work, or study, but you answer to me when I ask where you are and what you're doing. I need to know who you're with when you're not with me, or at work. No other man can touch you," I grind out. She's under my command now as I trail the fingers of my free hand up her inner thighs. The movement is slow, steady, and when I find her cunt, it's smooth and wet. She's already slick with arousal when I dip my fingers in, feeling her heat envelop me.

"Yes," she hisses in response.

"It means I can take you, fuck you, tease and taunt you, whenever and wherever I please. If I want to tie you up, whip you, cane you, I will. You will swallow my dick anywhere I want you to. Whether we're in private or public. But let me get one thing clear, Giana…" My voice trails off. The air hangs thickly over us with the impending threat I'm about to deliver. The rules and regulations that come with being mine swirl around us in a hazy cloud. "It doesn't matter where you are, or who you're with, you're mine. That means your mind and your body—every inch of it—is mine."

"What about my heart?"

Her question stills me. Do I want that? Can I take her heart without giving her mine in return? No, I can't. This is too much. I can't. Shoving her away, I step back. Her mouth parts in shock. Tears well in her eyes from my actions and I know it will only get worse.

Her heart is fragile, her mind even more so. I can't shatter her more than I already have. "Eli, I'm not asking for love." She takes a tentative step toward me, but I retreat. I can't have her touching me. She can't be near me. "Please? Don't do this. I didn't mean—"

"You want a fucking ring? Then find another little boyfriend down at the club because I'll never be that man." My words are sullen, filled with guilt at me even considering another woman. I can never replace Raquel.

"I don't want another man. I don't need a ring to tell me how you feel." She implores me, desperation emanates from every pore on her body.

"Get out. Take your shit and get out. Leave my shirt here. You need to leave." With that, I spin on my heel and exit the room. An anguished cry is wretched from her very core and it echoes through the hallway as I make my way to the East wing of the house.

Trying to block her out, I race into my bathroom and turn on the shower. I need to wash her scent from me. I can't have her sweetness near me. *What the fuck have I just done?*

GIANA

I don't remember the drive home. I don't remember what his driver said to me or how I managed to get into my apartment. Nothing makes sense. I don't know why it hurts. No, that's a lie, I know exactly why it hurts. What did I expect? He's still holding onto the pain from the past, and I didn't give him what he wanted. He asked for the truth and I didn't give it to him. Then again, he's not my boyfriend. I showed too much emotion too soon. I know he doesn't want that, he told me there's no chance of a relationship. No romance. No hearts and flowers.

When I called in sick today, Lei knew something was wrong immediately. Even though I told her I'm fine, that it was the flu, she didn't buy it. I guess that's what makes us such good friends. It's taken me years to get to this point, where he's finally given in and taken me home, and then I fucked it up. I should never have said anything.

Shaking my head, I focus on anything other than the memories that seem to invade my mind. Memories of him and me. That's all I have. I'm curled up on my bed. My body aches in delicious ways. My heart however, the agony in my chest is more than I can handle. I planned my attack, I knew I would get to him, but I didn't plan on him getting to me first.

Rolling over, I check the time and notice it's almost midday. I've been in a vegetative state since last night. When I walked into the apartment, emptiness settled over me and I cried. Tears fell for what I'd lost. Him. My pain kept me awake. I couldn't sleep because every time I close my eyes, I dreamed.

When three in the morning finally glowed angrily from my nightstand clock, I closed my eyes and forced the tears to cease. Awake or asleep, he's there. Both are as bad as each other, but none of them take me back in time, to last night, where I can swallow my words.

What made me ask him that? I know Elijah still loves his wife. It's evident. I'm an idiot. Sighing, I close my eyes and picture his face. That smile, those eyes that look right through me. Everything about him is all I need. There are times I used to wonder if I'd imagined him. If perhaps he was a figment of my imagination. Being with him again is surreal.

The desire to go online and stalk him rattles through me like an alcoholic needing their next drink. My body trembles at the thought of logging onto his social media accounts to see who he's talking to. If he's flirting with another toy who doesn't want his heart.

It's been almost twelve hours. I'd have counted the minutes but my mind is blank. All I see is him. Pushing up, I shove off the blankets and head straight for the shower. I've never allowed anyone in before, not like Elijah Draydon. He's broken me, and there's nothing I can do about it.

As soon as I step into the shower, a plan formulates in my mind. It's perfectly timed. As the idea settles, I smile. This time, I won't lose him. He walked away once, but I will not let him do it again. Being away from him

134   SINS OF SEVEN SERIES

last night was eye opening. It allowed me the space I need to make sure I don't fuck this up. I need to focus. I am in control.

I reaffirm this a few times while I scrub my skin clean from his scent. Soon, I'll have his spicy cologne on me forever. I need to give him honesty. He wants that, and I'll obey. I'll be the best submissive he's ever had, even better than Raquel. *Watch out Daddy, your toy is coming and she's going to make sure you're hers by the end of this week.*

Stepping into the offices of D&G Insurance two hours later, I find the desk where a receptionist should be sitting empty. "Hello. How can I—" The familiar deep rumble of Eli's partner comes from the office to my left. When I turn, the recognition on his face is one of surprise, but the smirk he offers tells me so much more. "Oh, the pretty girl from the coffee store."

"Hello, Sir," I purr like a kitten, which earns me a grin so wide and so goddamn handsome, I'm tempted to jump him right here, just to make Eli jealous.

"It's Oliver in the office," he informs me, offering a hand in my direction. When I take it, he gives mine a squeeze with fire dancing in his eyes.

"Well, Oliver, I overheard you're in need of a receptionist and I thought I'd come in for an interview." Hoping my voice sounds nonchalant, I smile.

"We do need someone in the office, yes. Come into my office, let's chat. Eli is in a meeting, but he'll be out soon."

I follow him into a cavernous room, furnished in dark wood and plush leather. "Is it a running theme between the two of you with the need for leather?" My question earns me a chuckle. Oliver turns to regard me. His eyes are like ice. Cold and gray. He's handsome in every respect. Dressed in a light blue dress shirt and black suit which fits him perfectly. The older man, possibly in his late thirties or early forties, looks like the mature version of a poster boy for the company.

"Leather is such a versatile fabric. Wouldn't you agree?" He gestures to the bright red chair opposite his desk.

"I do actually. The…" I allow my words to taper off as I stroke the arm of the chair, "feel of it is exquisite on bare skin." Lifting my gaze to meet his, I notice the way his Adam's apple bobs up and down with a swallow. I'm making him nervous and I wonder if it's because he may want me and he's nervous about Eli.

"Agreed, Ms…?"

"Ms. Bianchi," I respond with a small smile.

He nods, settling on the edge of his desk closer to me. His arms cross in front of his chest, causing the material to tighten around his biceps. For an older man who's got a smattering of salt and pepper to his hair, and soft crow's feet at the edge of his eyes, there's a sensuality about him. Control emanates from him. He's commanding attention, and I gladly give it to him.

"Let's talk work. Perhaps after, we can discuss the feel of leather on your creamy skin?" he murmurs seductively.

"Like fuck you will." The growl from behind me is feral, causing me to jump in the chair. Even though I know I should stand, I don't. He's playing right into my hand and I can't help smiling. *Well, well, well… Aren't you being an alpha male, Mr. Draydon?*

Oliver rises to his full height as Eli stalks into the office. A stand-off between two virile men. Both into dark, seductive delights, both could offer me all I need, but there's only one I want.

"Eli, nice to see you again." I smile, looking up at him, my words breaking the pissing contest between the two friends.

"Giana, go to my office," he bites out, his gaze never leaving Oliver's. "Now!" His no nonsense tone tells me I'm in big trouble. Just like I planned.

Pushing up, I step closer to the man who prefers Sir. Leaning up, I whisper in his ear. "I'd like to see what you can do with leather some time." With that, I turn and leave the two men to argue it out and step into Eli's office. An effortless plan, executed perfectly, and he fell for it. Hook, line, and sinker. I settle into a plush leather seat opposite a desk that's the complete opposite to Oliver's. It's decadent, beautiful, and it fits in the space perfectly.

It's not long when the door flies open. I rise and turn to regard the man who looks like he's about to emit lightning from his eyes and thunder from his mouth. "What the fuck are you thinking?"

Shrugging, I set my purse on his desk. "You said you wanted to offer me a job, I figured it would be better pay than the coffee shop and I can perhaps still continue my shifts at Sins."

"You were flirting with Oliver," he growls. "Do you think I'm stupid, Toy?"

"No, Daddy." My words are seductive, and I don't miss the desire written on his face. It's both beautiful and sensual. I want him to punish me. I crave for him to show me that I'm his. I want this man to own me.

"Jesus, Giana. What are you doing to me?" He's no longer angry. This time his words are anguished. His eyes, those beautiful golden orbs, gaze at me like I'm a prized possession.

"Just give me a job. You made it clear last night that we're no longer... That I'm not what you want. I spent the morning thinking about it and I need a job."

"You don't need a fucking job," he bites out while stalking toward me. There's dangerous lust swirling between us. The office is stifling with it, but I don't move. He reaches out and grips my hair, pushing me to my knees. "What you need is my dick in your throat." Without hesitation, I reach for his zipper and tug it down. Once my hand makes contact with his thick shaft, a growl falls from his lips. I pull his erection out, stroking it before flicking my tongue over the tip. His taste is my fix. And I take another hit.

Sucking him into my mouth, I revel in making this man crumble. His hands grip my head and his hips take control. His body moves against my face as he fucks my mouth, my throat. The crown of his cock enters my throat roughly, causing me to gag, but I take it like a good girl. My eyes lift to his and I find him staring down at me as he uses me.

"That's it, Toy. I want you. I fucking want you, Goddamnit." His gruff words are entangled with his hips as they slam against me, his abs hitting my nose. "Swallow my dick. Take it all. Show me how much you want to love me. How you want to give me your heart." His words both unsettle me and arouse me. With each command, he slams into my mouth, forcing himself into my throat, making me choke on his erection. "So fucking pretty when you cry." And I do. Tears of elation fall from my eyes.

He thinks he's in charge, but he's so wrong. I'm the one with the power. I may be on my knees, but I'm the one who's allowing him this pleasure. Suddenly, he pushes me off his cock. He steps back and crooks his finger, telling me with one small movement to stand and I do.

"Do you see me yet?" I question as I rise, wiping the saliva from my chin.

His cock still hard and ready for a good hard fucking. It juts out from between his thighs, making me lick my lips in anticipation. His glare is dark, devilish. "I've always known who you are sweet Giana, even though you've changed your name and your hair color. You'll always be the only girl my cock needs." A gasp falls from my lips when he smirks.

"You knew who I was when you saw me in the coffee shop," my voice drops to a murmur and his eyes light up with guilt. "Tell me, Eli? Since our time at the hospital you recognized me even though I'd colored my hair, changed my name. You knew it was me and all this time you acted as if I was a new toy to you."

"Did you think I wouldn't recognize the only woman who can swallow me like that without throwing up? The only woman who made me come so hard I saw forever in her eyes?"

His questions still me, right to the very core of who I am. I've needed him for so long, but he's always been away, unavailable. He's pushed me away once, walking out of a room and leaving me with nightmares. I gave up on a forever when he left. I didn't believe I was worth anything. But not this time.

"You knew it was me? Each time you walked into the coffee shop, every time you walked into Sins?" I ask with frustration heavily lacing my tone.

"Yes, I knew it was you. If I had come to you and confessed would you have taken me back right then and there? No." His admission does something to me. My heart leaps into my throat, threatening to choke me with emotion. I don't know if I should be happy or sad. Then he continues. "You hated me for walking out. I knew you did. At the time, you were a child."

"A child? I was eighteen. Even when you took my

body, when we first fucked you knew how I felt. I told you." He's right. I still hated him, but what he doesn't know is, I loved him too. "I loved you," I tell him honestly. The words scrape my throat raw with emotion. I shouldn't tell him, but it's time for honesty. If this is going to work between us, I need to give him everything.

"And I loved you," he confesses then and I see it's real. He's not lying. He really did love me as well. I thought I was just a game to him, a distraction, but he did love me.

"You walked out and didn't even give me a second thought. I was taken, bought and you didn't care. Is that how you love someone? Allowing them to be abused by someone that should have been locked in an asylum?" I want to hurt him, to make him see what he'd done to me. How he'd broken me once, and now, I have a feeling he's going to do it again. The only problem with loving someone so much is that you give them permission to hurt you. That's why we're so volatile. Dangerous and detrimental to each other.

"I didn't have a choice, Giana. They would have known. If I walked into your room that day to say goodbye, you'd have been in worse trouble than you could ever imagine. Your uncle wasn't the most understanding man. I was too old for you then, I still am. Only this time you're a grown woman rather than a child."

"I was eighteen!"

"I know. I just couldn't do it anymore. There was no way I could've given you a forever. You loved me too much and I needed to put space between us. I figured, if I left, you'd find a good boy your age."

"You still loved her, you still do." My accusation doesn't hurt him. It has agony spearing my chest. The heart that seems to only beat for him aches.

"I'll always love her." And there it is. My world shattered by four simple words. "But I love you too." Snapping my gaze to his, I search for a lie. I look for something that tells me he's only placating me, but there's nothing there.

"I know." My words are a whisper. His eyes shimmer with unbridled need. He yearns for me. His body is trembling and I know he's restraining himself.

"Why did you change your name?"

"Riley Giana Bianchi is my full name. I just never told you. When I needed a new life, I took my second name," I tell him, perching myself on the chair. My fingers tremble from nervous energy that skitters through me. I don't want him to send me away, but I also don't know what more we can do.

"Gia," he murmurs my name in a gravelly tone causing me to lift my eyes once more. "There's nothing more I want than to have you here. Near me all the time, but I need your absolute trust and honesty." He implores me with such ferocity my heart stutters. The expression on his face is everything my heart needs and more. He does love me. As much as I love him. If I want to do this, I have to give him everything. I nod slowly, twisting my hands in my lap. I allow my eyes to drift up to his and then I do it. I give him the words I've been too afraid to say all this time.

"I'm still sick," I confess because it's the truth. He knows what happened to me. Well... most of it. When I was admitted, I sat in bed when the realization hit me that I'm an addict.

Not drugs or alcohol, but men.

Sex. I hungered for it. I needed the pain.

That's why when I first met Eli at the tender age of seventeen, I let him touch me, kiss me. When I finally turned eighteen, I begged him to fuck me and make me cry and he did. It was like getting high every time he came to my room. The doctors' thought he was my boyfriend. They didn't care either way.

I meet his gaze, and tell him earnestly. "I'm still an addict. It's still in my veins, Eli. How can you want someone so… broken? So fucked up."

He shakes his head, stares at me for a long while, before pulling me into his arms. "You're no sicker than I am," he murmurs against my hair, planting a kiss so gentle yet so commanding. It says *mine.* "I took advantage of you." My attempt at refusing his words is hindered by him holding my head against his chest. The beat of his heart thrums against my ear.

"I was taken advantage of long before you ever came along, Mr. Draydon. And when you left… It was my nightmare. I was in hell where you left me." He steps back, hands on my shoulders as he watches me. His golden eyes spark with emotion. Anger. Fury. And I know it's from my confession.

Resignation on his features tells me he's about to request something I can't comply with. He's going to ask for the truth. I know he'll want to know everything. Why I was in the hospital, what happened after he left. And most of all, he's going to find out what a shattered toy I really am.

I want us to work. I need it. I don't know if I can go through it again, to relive the memories, those vile images in my head that make me the way I am, but for him, I'll try.

The images I'm about to relive make me need the dark, the pain that allows me, forces me to allow myself to recall what happened. It takes me to a place in my head where I'm safe. I meet those beautiful orbs that seem to look right through me. And then, as always, he doesn't ask, he commands. "Tell me about it. I want to know everything."

ELEVEN

ELIJAH

She's silent for too long. I've asked for the truth. One I know she'll have trouble talking about. Not because she doesn't want to, but because she can't go back there in her mind. I spoke to the doctor and found out a lot about this little girl. Her pain. Her nightmares.

It's been almost five years since I last saw her in that hospital room. When I forced my way into her life. We became friends. Strange, but true. Each day she'd find me in the communal garden, and we'd talk about everything and nothing at all. She'd tell me her naughty secrets and I'd tell her mine.

The first time we fucked was in a dark hallway in the stairwell of the institution. She was in there because she tried to commit suicide. Her mind was in tiny fragments at my feet and I took her, I fucked her until she couldn't think straight, and it was in that moment she seemed to pick up those tiny shards and piece them together.

She found solace in the depravity of what we did. I choked her, I rammed myself into her tight cunt. She clawed at me, ripping the skin until I bled for her. We were animals. And we loved every second. I took my pain out on her and she took her anger out on me.

"I think we took advantage of each other. Your wife died and I taunted you for a year before you finally allowed your animal loose on me," she murmurs. I don't respond for a moment so she continues. "I didn't realize you were a crazy asshole."

"I didn't think you were a psychopathic bitch." I grin. "But I looked for you, I searched for a year. You disappeared. How did you find me?" I ask, wondering how after all this time, she was the one who found me and not the other way around.

"For you, I would have done anything. It took time. When I escaped the clutches of a sadistic monster, I ran until I found Carrick and Seven Sins. I got the job at the coffee shop to make extra money, then Rick offered me a job at the club. After the first time, you walked in and didn't recognize me, I kept hoping one day you'd see me. I need you, Eli."

I nod. I need her too but I didn't want to admit she was the same girl. Every day I saw this beautiful brunette, denying myself the chance to once again see her platinum blonde hair that I loved fisting while I drove into her tight body.

"If we do this… if there's a chance we can make this work, you're mine." She nods at my words. She's been mine since I first took her cunt at eighteen. She's also been mine since I ate her out until her legs shook so much she couldn't stand.

"You promised no hearts, but—"

"You've given me yours. Haven't you?" My question has her looking at me with wariness and I realize that it's my fault. I pushed her away when she showed emotion. For a moment, she doesn't respond. Then she affirms with a nod what I already knew. "We were supposed to move on. You were meant to go study, find a life of your own. A boy who would be able to make you happy."

"I have found my life. It's here with you. Don't send me away again." She pleads with me then and I can't deny her anything. Not when she pins me with those big doe eyes that hold so much love for me. The truth of who she really is, what she really went through still needs to be discussed. Before we get to that, I'm going to make sure she's safe.

She wants this.

I want this.

She'll be Daddy's Toy.

"If you stay with me then that's it. No more fucking around, you quit your job at the club. No other Dom, no other Master will get to see you the way I do. If you want to go to Seven Sins, then you will do so as mine. Are we clear?"

"Yes, Daddy," she quips playfully. We're both fucked up in so many ways, but we're perfectly matched in others. Since the day I first saw her, I was drawn in by her beauty, her innocence, and her smile. She never showed her true self to anyone other than me. It was the one thing that made me go back every day. I needed good in my life after Raquel died, and Riley, or Giana was it.

"Now, you better get to your desk and start going through the mail. Make sure Oliver and I don't miss any meetings," I order, but all she offers is a smile. No sassiness from her today. She spins on her four-inch heels and stalks out of my office with her hips swaying suggestively. This woman will be my fucking downfall because I want to fuck her right here, right now.

The door opens before she reaches it and Oliver stalks in. His gaze flits between Gia and I as he regards us warily. "I didn't hear any screaming so I figured it's safe to come in?" My best friend stands on the threshold of my office with a grin on his face. With a quick glance at Giana as she passes him, he only offers a nod before turning to me and steps further into the office.

"What do you want?"

"This girl…" He lowers his voice. When the door shuts behind him, he asks the question I know he's been dying to since he first saw Giana. "Is it her? The one you told me about?" I nod. "I thought you said she's blonde?"

"Was blonde," I correct him. "She colored her hair. Her appearance has changed from the seventeen-year-old I first met."

"And you're sure she's the one?"

Settling in my office chair, I regard him with a nod. "Yes. I've never been so sure in my life. Unless she's playing a game, but somehow, I doubt it."

"You're claiming her then?"

"I am. I've just made it clear to her that she's to leave her job at Sins. If she does want to visit, she'll go as mine. No other man will have her." He smirks, nodding knowingly. I've never laid claim to any of the toys he and I have shared. "I'm still going ahead with my plan though," I tell him. I know he doesn't agree with my plan to find her uncle, but he'll have to get over it. When I find the asshole who hurt her, I'm going to make sure his body is never found. And if it is, it won't be in one piece.

"I'm not telling her shit, man. You just be careful. If she's as volatile as you say, then you need to remember that she'll lose it if she finds out what you're doing."

Pushing off the seat, I place both hands on the desk. He may be my best friend, but I'm not averse to punching him the fuck out. "I'm not a child. I know what I'm doing."

"I don't doubt you, Elijah. Just remember, once she's claimed, you're going to have to deal with the repercussions of her personality."

"Aren't you late for a meeting?" The asshole chuckles, shaking his head, he opens the door and steps out into the reception area.

"See you later, sweet girl." Even though he fucked me off, I know he's right. I searched high and low for her, but could never pinpoint where she was. Until the day I walked into the coffee shop and the brunette looked at me with those same dark eyes that took me right back to the night she kneeled before me in the dingy stairwell, and inhaled my cock like it was her last meal.

I was too old for her. At least that's what I told myself. I even convinced myself that I was mourning Raquel's death and I'd get over the little toy. But I didn't. Each month that passed I got more and more addicted to her, to the memory of her. I fucked countless women, used them, made them cry and scream, but none compared to Giana. At least, her name wasn't Giana then, it was Riley.

Sitting back, I shut my eyes and recall the day I first

saw her.

"Hello." My voice carries through the room. One small single bed sits against the wall and the little girl lying on it is a waif. Beautiful, her long golden hair the color of sunshine. Big brown eyes peer at me.

"What do you want?" An angry response comes from the innocent face.

Chuckling, I step into the room and settle myself in the chair beside the bed. "Nothing, I'm just bored and I was wandering the hallways."

When she shifts, the thin gown they've given her to wear rides up slim thighs. "Are you a patient or a visitor?" she asks.

"A visitor. My wife is in the next ward." The words hurt to voice, but I tell her anyway. She doesn't tell me she's sorry, she doesn't apologize for my wife being ill. Instead, she shrugs. We don't say anything for a while and I feel the need to explain why I'm sitting in her room. "I just wanted to see why you look so sad."

"What makes you think I'm sad?" She sits up then, crossing her legs, offering me a glimpse at the black panties that cover her cunt. "Do you like looking at me down there?"

Lifting my gaze, I smirk, knowing full well she caught me. I meant for her to. "I do. I'm sure it's a pretty little pussy." My words don't shock her. They should've, but she only stares at me as if she's used to men talking to her like that.

It angers me. I want to be the only man who talks to her like a toy. "I suppose it's average. I mean… I don't go around comparing mine with other girls."

Her response makes me laugh. There's a soft pink on her cheeks, not of embarrassment, it's desire swirling in her dark eyes.

"Why are you in here?" I steer the conversation away from her body. Mainly because I'm hard, I'm rock solid for this girl when I shouldn't be. When I should be sitting watching the life support system that keeps my wife alive beep. She's no longer coherent. She's a vegetable and I'm the selfish asshole keeping her alive with a machine.

"I wanted to die," the little toy says.

"Why? You're young, you have your whole life ahead of you." Once again, she shrugs. I want to spank her. I want to punish her for not answering me. But most of all, I want to fuck her. I want to see her pouty lips wrap around the base of my cock.

156

"Not everyone wants to live the life given to them. What if you were dealt an existence of pain, agony, and heartache?"

"You're too young to know about those kinds of things, Doll." Her eyebrows shoot up at the nickname, but she doesn't say anything about it. Instead she watches me with an intensity that tells me there's more to this little toy than meets the eye.

"Being young doesn't stop what happens to someone. Age is only a number, I'm a girl, I'm a dirty toy." Her words have my heart stilling in my chest. She's not just saying it, she believes it. Someone must have hurt her.

"What happened to you?"

We sit silently as she thinks about what to say next. I can feel the wheels turning in her mind. Spinning on an endless loop of memories. I'm sure the images she hides are gruesome. And I know if she tells me what they are, I may commit murder.

I push up to leave, but she reaches for my hand. I don't move, I don't breathe. I wait for her to tell me. To give me her honest answer. "Life happened to me."

I sneak a glance over my shoulder, meeting endless dark pools. "Me too. Maybe we can die together."

My suggestion earns me a pretty smile. It's not faked, it's genuine, like the way her hand tightens around my wrist.

"Then come find me when you're ready to find your fate."

Shaking my head of the memory, I can't help feeling that familiar emotion that I've locked away for so long. Love. It was her who gave me purpose. She made me realize that dying wasn't an option. Even though I thought that ending my life would allow me to be with the wife I lost, I knew deep down I couldn't go through with it. Instead of physically dying, I died emotionally and it's because of her that I was alive. I chose the fire she gave me, instead of the cold emptiness that overtook me time and again.

Giana was always there. In each face I fucked, in every cunt I drove into, and on every inch of flesh I marked with my hand, whip, and cane. She was the one I was punishing. It was always her and somehow I knew it.

The other thing I didn't realize is that night I had implanted my cold dead heart in her hands. And all these years she kept it safe. "Are you ready to go home, Daddy?"

I glance up and realize it's been almost an hour that

I've been lost in the memories.

"Always, Toy. With you... Always."

TWELVE

GIANA

I'm nervous. This could go either way. Once he knows what happened, he can either be appalled, or he'd want to get revenge for me. Sitting here, I feel like a teenager once more. As if he's taken me back to when I was seventeen and he was thirty. I'm completely naked, he asked me to strip as soon as we got into the house, but he's gone and I'm kneeling on the floor waiting. It's always the anticipation that makes my body tingle. Knowing he can do anything he wants to me, but not knowing when he will do it.

My heart hammers in my chest, my mouth is dry, and as my tongue licks my lips, I find myself thirsty, not for a drink, but for him. I want this man. I'm finally

160

going to have him and I know I'll be okay. I need to offer him the honesty he deserves. It's the only way we'll be able to move forward.

When the door finally clicks, then slides open, I feel him step into the room. "Hello, sweet girl." The rough timber of Oliver sends my nerves into disarray.

"Hello, Sir," I respond as I'm meant to. I want to look up, to see his face, but I know it will earn me a punishment. The heat of Eli is behind me. His body is like a cocoon, which warms me. Shiny black shoes move into my vision.

"Eyes up, pretty."

When I lift my gaze, I'm met with the steel eyes of Oliver Michaelson. He offers me one of his signature smirks when he crouches down. Once we're eye level, he reaches for my chin, and lifting it, he regards me for a moment.

"Are you nervous?" He asks in a rough tone. I shake my head. "Do you want me to watch Eli fuck you?" His words are laced with desire, hunger, and need.

"Yes, Sir," I respond, not recognizing my own voice. I didn't know he'd be here, and clearly this is why Eli had taken so long to come to me. He was waiting for Oliver to arrive. I don't know what this test is meant to accomplish, but I trust Elijah with all I have.

"Good girl," he coos, running his finger over my lower lip with his thumb. Then his touch is gone. He rises to full height, heading to the chair on the other side of the room. Just out of my direct sight.

"Stand." My Daddy's voice is gruff.

I obey, rising to my feet, but I don't turn to face him. Instead, I watch Oliver unbutton his crisp white shirt. He tugs it out of the waistband of his black slacks, leaving it open. His body is bared to my gaze. His chest has a smattering of hair, but he's toned. Not chiseled like those male models, but beautiful to the eye. And for an older man, it's clear he looks after himself.

"Do you want Oliver to taste your pussy?" Eli asks from behind me. His cock presses against the cheeks of my ass.

This must be turning him on more than I thought. "Only if you request it, Daddy."

Oliver smirks from the corner where he's now comfortably seated. The sinful way his gaze rakes over me has me shuddering with an innate need to feel his mouth on me. "I think my Toy would like for you to taste her, Oliver. I'll watch." Before Elijah has time to move, the man before me rises from the seat and stalks toward me like I'm his dessert and he's about to devour me in one bite.

He shoves his shirt from his torso, allowing it to pool on the floor. Crooking his finger, he summons me closer. I didn't notice the sofa behind me before, but when I'm turned around, I see Eli on the one end, seated like king of the castle as he watches his best friend lead me toward him.

My stomach flip flops with nerves when Oliver settles beside Daddy and calls me over. "I want you to get up on the sofa, position that bare little hole on my face and ride me like you're riding your Daddy's dick."

His filthy words send me spiraling into the abyss of depravity. The ache between my legs intensifies until all I can think about is an orgasm. Until my blood is boiling, painfully racing through my veins. I cast one quick glance at Eli who nods. He's giving me permission. So, I step up onto the sofa, my legs on either side of Oliver's body.

His hands reach up, gripping my thighs as he positions me where he wants me. A flattened tongue laps at my throbbing core and I cry out. "Ride my face, little Toy. I want your sweet essence all over my face." Sir orders from below me and I do, my hips buck as I take what I need from him.

My hands grip the back of the sofa to hold myself steady because if I don't I'm afraid I might fall over. His mouth sucks on my clit, his teeth graze the bundle of nerves, and I'm teetering on the edge. Right on the precipice of a release so intense I'm sure I'll pass out.

Hands on my ass still me for a moment, when I glance over my shoulder I find Daddy gripping both cheeks, opening me to his gaze. "I'm going to lick this little ass while you come on Oliver's face," he informs me in a seductive tone. I don't know how much more I can handle, but when Sir's fingers find my core, dipping into the wetness, a keening mewl falls from my lips. I'm wet, drenched. My body is theirs to use, to play with until they're both satisfied. As much as I should be ashamed of loving both men taking me like this, I'm not, it's the most erotic thing I've ever felt and I can't say no.

Fingers probe my puckered entrance and I freeze momentarily. The last time I had someone take me there it was the worst pain I'd ever felt in my life. Not the pleasurable kind. It was agony, and I wished for death. Since then, it's always been off limits. The dark memories of what happened to me still ghost my mind, taunting me.

"Calm down, Toy. It's me," Daddy coos from behind me, while Oliver's rough hands grip my thighs, holding me steady over his mouth. My eyes roll back as four fingers enter me. Two in my pussy and two in my ass.

Both scissor me open. Teasing my holes, making me pliable to their ministrations. "Oh God!" I cry out when Oliver bites down on my clit. The sensation shoots through every nerve in my body and I come violently. My pussy pulses wildly around his fingers and my ass tightens around Daddy's fingers. I can't stand, my knees are wobbly, but I'm being held up somehow. I lose all sense of time as both men devour me. Tongues, fingers, and hands.

Both of their mouths are on me. Unrelenting. Giving

me more pleasure than I'd ever had. The experience of having two men worship me like this has emotion tightening in my chest, gripping me painfully. Tongues, fingers, warm, wet mouths eat me, lick me, and fuck me until release after release slams into me. I'm not sure how many I have, but my mind is blank from the past, from the memories. All that exists is the here and now.

I'm merely a plaything for them. A toy. Daddy's toy. I smile then. I've finally got what I wanted. Eli is mine. After all these years, I'm finally his.

As I come down from the high of my orgasms, I find myself being lowered onto a thick, hard erection. The man before me, Sir, is staring at me like I'm an ornament. Like I'm fragile and he's afraid to break me. His mouth comes down on my one peaked nipple. He suckles it playfully, flicking his tongue over the bud. When he grazes his teeth over it, I grip his hair, holding him against my chest.

"Naughty Toy." A growl from behind me startles me and I release Oliver from my grip. A swat on my ass stings erotically and I move my hips. "You're going to take us both, right now." A warning. The cold lubricant on my ass tingles as Daddy teases it at my tight hole. Once again, he works two fingers inside me until I'm loose. At least, loose enough to take his cock.

Then I feel it. The crown nudging against me, requesting more. I nod. He pushes. My body slowly accepts the thickness as he pushes into my ass. The pain sears me, but the pleasure of Oliver sends me into orbit as both men start moving. I know for a fact that Daddy's cock isn't fully seated or I'd have passed out from the pain.

We're a trinity of bodies moving in sync. Grunts of pleasure, moans of delight, and slapping of skin is all I hear as we all three move together, hoping to find the release that slowly beckons. It won't take long. I'm almost there.

"Such a good toy for Daddy and Sir, aren't you baby?"

Nodding, because I can't find the words, I feel the smile on his face. I don't know who. I have no idea where the words come from. My body is a vessel for them. They take and I give. But as much as I do allow, they give me more than I've ever thought possible.

People may see me as a slut. As a whore. But this is my love. This is my body. And I am owned. Happiness warms my chest as both men plunge inside me. Filling me with not only their cocks, but their love. They give me everything in return for my body.

"Come for us, Toy. Scream for us."

I do. Someone pinches my clit and the other tweaks and twists my nipples as their hips piston into me.

Pain.

Pleasure.

Euphoria.

THIRTEEN

ELIJAH

She's innocent, yet seductive. When she finally fell asleep in our arms, I laid her down on the bed and watched her for a moment until I knew I needed to get some rest myself. The threesome was a test. I needed to see if she really trusted me. I wouldn't allow any other man near her, but Oliver is someone I trust with my life.

He's spent years training submissives and Dominants alike, so his suggestion at us sharing her first didn't sit well with me. But when he explained that it's a test of trust. She's been hurt before, but if she really was submitting fully, she'd do anything to please me. Also, she'd allow herself to trust fully. Completely. If she'd called out a safe word, I would have stopped, but

I needed to know her heart was in this, not just her body and mind.

That sweetness she exudes, is her game. She plays it well, like a virgin taunting her first lover. Oliver left not too long ago and since he walked out, I've been thinking about his advice to get the truth from her. I know I need to know what happened to her after I left, but deep down, I'm scared. I don't want to lose her, and I think if I push, she's going to walk out. I should man up and talk to her. She's explosive though. Her personality is volatile. But after tonight, I know at least she trusts me.

I gave into Oliver's suggestion of a threesome to confirm in my fucked-up mind that she'd be willing to do anything for me. Even though I knew she would. There wasn't a question about it.

The phone buzzing on the sofa beside me drags my attention away from her. A message from my best friend. A thank you for the night. He knew, and he was right about what would happen. The threesome was intense, and it allowed her to offer me more trust than I'd expected. Now all that's left is for me to make sure she tells me what I need to know.

Pushing up, I head out to the kitchen and pour a large shot of gin. Not my regular drink of choice, but I need something different. Perhaps it's a bad idea, I need a clear head when it comes to Giana. I want to call her by her real name, but I don't know if that would go down well. She's hiding from her past, her demons that seem to have followed her into the present.

"Do you ever sleep?" Turning to find the beautiful vision of a naked Giana staring at me from the entrance to the living room, I can't help smiling.

"I do, but after a session like that, I'm a little wound up." Lifting the glass, I tip it toward her. As she pads over to me, her breasts bounce with every step. Her nipples are a dusky-rose, having hardened into little peaks that my mouth waters to taste. I want to suck them and bite down, causing her to cry out. The sound of her whimpers and moans I now own and I realize I'm the luckiest man in the world. She's mine. My toy.

"Can I help ease that?" Her sultry voice is all I need to hunger for her again. As much as I want to fuck her, I know we need to talk. There's so much we need to say to each other. So many truths need to be confessed.

"How about you tell me about what happened to you, sweetheart?" I've never been so loving to any woman I've had in my house. After or before Raquel.

"Do we need to do that right now?" Giana questions with a seductive smirk that tells me she'd rather be swallowing my dick than talking.

Setting my glass down, I nod. "We do." My murmur has her face falling into a sexy pout. I reach for her, lifting her against me, I walk us toward the sofa and settle on it with her straddling my lap. This isn't the best position to keep my concentration, but it will keep her happy while she tells me what she suffered through.

"You're serious, aren't you?" she questions then, realizing I'm not letting up this time, no matter how much she taunts me. I nod in response. My heart thuds against my rib cage. I'm not sure I want to know, because I don't doubt I'll be planning a murder once she's confessed. Her gaze darts away, trailing over everything in the room but me. "I was thirteen when I was broken for the first time. He broke me. He forced himself inside my ass, he didn't do anything to make the pain stop. He told the nurses he'd found me like that when he came home."

Her words are filled with anguish that I feel right to my core. My hands are splayed on her hips, holding her as if I'm her anchor. Giving her the support she needs, I allow her to lean in, her head on my chest. I want to cocoon her from pain, from heartache. Like a father would his daughter, only, this is much more sordid than that. I'm her Daddy Dom, the man she's supposed to rely on. To satisfy both her sexual needs, as well as emotional. A father figure, but with the sexual benefits of a boyfriend.

When I chose the path I'd follow, becoming a Dominant, I didn't realize how caring I would be. At first, I enjoyed the sadist side, like Oliver. But as time went on and I learned more about who I was, I knew I couldn't dole out pain without pleasure. I wasn't as fucked in the head as Oliver is. I know why he is the way he is, but deep down, I'm not like that. I'm caring, gentler in other respects, whereas he's cold from the way he fucks to his professional life.

She's silent for a long while and I realize I got lost in my thoughts. I know she's not looking at me because it makes it more difficult for her to tell me what happened while facing me. Her body is warm as it molds to mine.

"I was a pretty girl, at least that's what he told me the first time. My parents had gone out to their anniversary dinner and they asked my uncle to babysit even though I was far from a baby. I'd never been out with a boy, but I knew about sex, and…" A soft sigh falls from her lips, filled with apprehension. "We were sitting on the sofa watching one of my favorite TV shows when he put his hand on my thigh. At first, I pushed it away, thinking it's weird, but he said he was just showing me how much he loved me."

"Giana—"

"Then he pushed me down on the floor. He told me I was so pretty, that pretty girls were like dolls. They needed to be played with. In one way, I knew what was happening, and in another, I didn't realize that I'd be broken beyond recognition. Not physically, but emotionally. Everything seemed to blur together, me pushing him away, him grunting. It's a sound that stayed with me for years. The pain. It felt like I was being torn in two. There was so much blood." She's speaking in short sentences, taking deep breaths in between. The wetness from her eyes soak the shirt I'm wearing and my arms wrap around her, cocooning her as if I can shelter her from the agony.

"Giana, stop." It's an order she has to obey. "You are mine. You're safe. I will never hurt you like that."

"After a few months of him doing it, I became numb. I went to school and sought out other boys who would love me. Maybe in my mind I figured if they did things to me, I'd find love. A girl with a hungry heart always believes love comes from physical contact." She laughs then, mirthless and unamused. "At least that's what the psychiatrists said."

"Look at me." She does, and when she lifts her gaze to mine, I see the love shining in them. She loves me. "Why did you try to kill yourself?"

When she blinks for a moment too long, I think she's about to shut down, but then she opens those soulful eyes and spears me right through the heart. "I wanted the pain to stop. I wanted him to stop." She shrugs. "When you came along, it changed. I found something worth living for until you walked away," she says. It's not meant to make me feel guilty but it does. Then she looks at me again. "After you left, I was… I was *sold* to someone. A Master, is what he called himself. I thought he'd give me the love you took, but he didn't. He wasn't like you, he was… He was sick." She sighs, and it's filled with pure agony. "He violated me in more ways than I can count."

"Riley." Her name slips from my lips and she gasps. "I'm sorry, Giana. I just… I didn't mean to leave you. I thought I was doing what was the best for you."

"I escaped the monster after two years. I slept on the sidewalks, under bridges for three or four months until I met Carrick. Even though he saved me, I took a blade to both my wrists. Rick found me when I was late for a meeting and gave me hell. He whipped me because he didn't know what else to do with me. When I told him why, he cared for me and healed me in his own way."

"You fucked Carrick?" She shrugs like it's nothing. I suppose after all she's been through, it might not mean much to her. "Why me, Gia?"

"I love you, Eli," she confesses. It's easy, there's no tension in her body.

I thought she ran away from home. Figured her parents didn't notice, but clearly what I knew of this girl wasn't the truth. When I did search for her, there was nothing on her. Her family didn't care, and now I know why. No police reports, no missing person's posters, just… nothing.

"You were twenty when you escaped that monster?" I hiss in angry frustration.

"I was." She affirms like it's an obvious occurrence for a teenager to go through the hell that she did and then try to kill herself. "It's been years since you walked out and I've been through both hell and heaven. Since I found you, I knew I needed to find the courage to tell you who I really was. I spent years locked in his dungeon. He'd feed me a bare minimum to keep me alive and strong enough to take the beatings. To take his cock in all my holes. It was… normal to me."

"Why did you try to hurt yourself when you were safe? Carrick would never hurt you." This was the question I'd been dying to ask. Why try to kill yourself when there's people who would care for you? Why not focus on healing and giving life a chance?

"I wanted someone to find me. To finally care and Carrick did," she whispers painfully, lifting her gaze, she blinks and a lone tear races down her cheek. I'm tempted to lick it, tasting her sorrow, and allowing it to seep into my veins. "I wanted someone to finally see me." Her words cause a crack in my chest, so wide open, it's festering with hatred and anger at three people who were meant to keep her safe. The words she implored me with only yesterday, *just see me,* settle heavily in my chest. I do see her.

Her naked body trembles, wracking with sobs.

"When you looked at me in that hospital room, it was the first time I felt like someone was actually seeing me." Her confession has emotion tightening in my throat. Thickening, attempting to choke me. If only she knew how much I saw. How much of me I saw in her.

"I'll always see you, Toy. Always." She nuzzles into my chest then, as if she's trying to burrow inside me. Like she wants to hide from the world and I'm her knight in shining armor. Only, I'm not the savior. I'm the one who could ruin her worse than anyone else in her life. Not because I want to, but because she's in love with me.

Closing my eyes, I inhale her scent. Her warmth is all consuming. It's embedded into my soul. "Why do you like the pain?" I question; my brows furrow when I realize how much agony she's been put through, yet she loves when I inflict pain on her.

"It's the only time I feel alive. It makes me realize I'm free, I'm living, and I'm wanted. If you didn't love me, you wouldn't hurt me. With each kind of love, comes a variation of pain." Her words are dark, yet so damn true.

I do love her. I love her more than my next breath. "And you're so sure I love you?" I question as her head snaps up. She meets my gaze, seeing the gentle amusement I watch her with. Then she nods confidently.

"If you didn't love me, you would never have let me stay here. None of your other toys have ever spent the night with you. Yet, here I am." Her mouth quirks into a satisfied smirk. She reads me like a book. Open and bare to her gaze.

"Well done, sweet girl. Now, I need to be inside you. Take my dick out." Her hands work quickly as she unzips my slacks and pulls my cock free. It's thick and hard, ready to slide into her tight heat.

"Can I suck you first?"

Chuckling, I shake my head. "No, rub your cunt on me, just those pretty lips, Toy. Back and forth, I want to feel you coat me with your juices." Her hips move. My hands grip her hips as she undulates over my erection. Her sweet cunt drips all over my shaft, my slacks, and I revel in the sensation of her body sliding over mine.

Soft, sweet moans fall from her lips as she takes pleasure. She's using me as I want to use her. I'll never hurt her, only in pleasure. I suppose that's the kind of love we have. She's my baby girl, my toy, and I'll always be her Daddy.

FOURTEEN

GIANA

"Wake up, Giana," he murmurs in my ear, and a small smile curls my lips. The heat of his breath fans over my cheek, causing my skin to dot with goose bumps. Rolling over, I open my eyes to find Eli staring down at me.

"Am I late?" I ask, my voice croaky with sleep and heavy with emotion. He shakes his head, but the way he's regarding me tells me there's something he's hiding. "What's wrong, Eli?" Scooting up, I wait for it. I expect him to tell me to leave, to take my shit and go. Like every other man in my life, the disappointment has been something I've dealt with.

"I made breakfast, I'd like you to come downstairs.

We need to talk before heading into the office." He leans in, the clean scent of his aftershave is spicy and masculine. Reminding me of why all those years ago I found solace in his arms.

"I'll be right down."

"I want you clean shaven, smooth and warm. I've laid out an outfit for you in the closet. And remember the garter belt." He smirks, pushes off the bed, and heads out of the bedroom. We slept in the guest room last night after my confession and after we had sex. My gaze darts around, taking in the soft feminine furnishings that certainly don't suit him.

Swinging my legs over the edge of the mattress, I pad over to the en suite bathroom and step inside. It's immaculate. The white Italian tiles are patterned with a light shadow of blue. Almost as if I'm standing in the clouds, with the sky all around me. There's a his and hers basin, as well as a corner tub with jets that remind me of a Jacuzzi.

The shower could probably fit three or four people, causing me to wonder if he ever did that with other toys. Jealousy has always been my weakness, but this is something different. I'm in love with this man and the thought of him with anyone else sets my blood boiling.

Stepping into the shower, I turn on the taps and allow the cool water to wake me up from the sleepy state of my brain. My body trembles from the cold, but as the spray heats, I warm immediately. Closing my eyes, I recall the memories that kept me going through the five years without Eli.

I was seventeen when we met. He made me come on his hand before my eighteenth birthday. For months, we were just friends. Talking everyday about things that didn't matter. He gave me life, he offered me the attention that no one else ever gave me. And I reveled in it. I watched him mourn. I saw him cry. As a young girl, you don't ever expect to see an adult crying, but he did. I was his rock as much as he was mine, but mostly, I think I was his solace as he was mine. There was a connection even then. Before I knew what it was, I loved him.

At that age, all I knew was pain, heartache, and the horror of being used. Men abused me, boys took what they could, even when I didn't want to give it.

"Hi." He stalks into the room. There's a limp in his gait.

"Did you hurt yourself?" I quiz him, lifting my chin in gesture to his leg.

Through narrowed eyes, he stares at me for a moment. The cigarette between my lips gets pulled away. He tells me I shouldn't do it. Every day, each week he comes back here and he warns me that it's bad for me.

I don't listen. Why should I listen to a man I don't know? "Why do you do it?" He asks with frustration dripping from every word.

Shrugging, I smile up at him. "Because nobody else cares."

"I do."

Those two small words are foreign to me. I've never heard someone say them. It's one of those things I've always been in tune with. If someone says they care, they're lying.

It's how grown-ups make us do what they want. Force. It's part of life.

"Come, we're going for a walk."

"I don't like being alone with men, but why am I okay with you?" I ask.

He doesn't look at me, merely shrugs as if I just told him

about the weather.

The grounds are quiet. He always comes at night, not when it's completely dark, but those moments between the sun setting on the horizon and the moon finally making itself known. Casting a silvery light on everything below, I glance up and stare at the sliver that greets us tonight.

"They said I could go home soon."

It's a lie. He knows it is. "Look." He points in front of us. It's a small greenhouse on the edge of the garden. "Let's go and have a look." I follow him out to the glass building. He opens the door, allowing me to step inside. It's humid, making my chest feel almost heavy.

The plants are beautiful, flowers of every color shimmer under the dim light. I'm lost in thought when I feel him behind me. His warmth. The spicy scent of his cologne. He smells like a man, like a good man.

"You're not scared of me. Are you?"

"No," I respond honestly. His hands on my hips don't make me cringe. Instead they make my body tingle. Especially between my legs. He trails his fingertips lightly up my arms, causing me to shudder. His lips are warm and soft on my neck. The soft suckling of his mouth has my blood heating.

"I'm going to make you come on my fingers." Fear skitters down my skin. I want to say no. To protest, but it doesn't make a difference. He's a man, he'll take it anyway. "Tell me no. If you don't want it then say it."

"Men take. Even when I say no."

He spins me around in his grip, his normally golden eyes darken considerably, even though we're in the dimly lit building. "I will never, ever force myself on you. Do you understand me? If you say no, then I'll stop. I just… I want you, Riley. You're beautiful and I want to get lost in you."

His words are too emotional, so I spin around, my back to his chest. "Then make me come."

Tentatively, his hands roam my body. "Hold my hands, I want you to use me for your pleasure." His words cause me to gasp, but I place my hands on his and we explore my frame together. When I finally take one hand and lead him to where I need it, where my body quivers and pulses, his fingers dip into the material. Pressing against my mound. The delight shoots through me.

My head drops back on his shoulder and a moan, whimper, then a keening mewl falls from me. It is pleasure. I've never felt such intensity. An ache that grips me in its fierce hold, keeping *me on the edge. I shift our hands up and then down, under the material of my shorts to find the wetness between my thighs.*

"Jesus Christ, you're soaked," he growls. Actually fucking growls like an animal, and I push one thick digit into my hole. Into the tightness of my body. "Fuck my hand, baby. I want you to come all over my fingers. Come for me, Toy."

It was the first time he called me that, and I cry out as my orgasm tears through me. Sending me over the edge of bliss. My hips slow, his mouth is still on my neck as he whispers.

"You're exquisite."

"Thank you," my voice is a raspy whisper. He pulls his fingers from my core and brings them to his mouth. I watch transfixed as he licks the wetness from his fingers.

"And you're delicious." His tongue darts out, tasting every drop of the glistening juices from his fingers. It's both erotic and filthy, but it makes me smile.

"Next time, it's my turn." I try to saunter past him, but his hand reaches out, tugging me against him.

"Next time, I'm tasting it right from the source."

Opening my eyes, I realize the water is ice cold. "Was that a good memory?" The deep rumble comes from the doorway after I've shut off the taps.

When I step out of the shower, he hands me a white fluffy towel that's big enough to wrap around my body twice. "It was actually. Do you remember the greenhouse?"

"How could I forget? It was the first time I tasted that sweet cunt. You drenched my fingers with your delicious juices." Pulling me against him, he leans in to plant a soft kiss on my lips. "Come on, we need to hurry. You took too long in the shower."

"What did you want to talk to me about?" I realize my question has desperation and trepidation all over it. I don't want to say goodbye to him, but deep down, I know if I fuck this up he'll walk away. I need to keep my secret. Even though I've been wanting to tell him since the day he first touched me, I know I can't.

I can't lose him. I'll never survive.

FIFTEEN

ELIJAH

"Tell me what happened?" Her voice is a whisper of sweetness and innocence.

I don't know why I come here every day, but I can't help myself. She's become an addiction. Just to see her is something that plays on my mind. And when I leave her at night, I miss her. It's ridiculous. She's a child.

"She told me to let her go. I had to turn the machines off and walk away." The truth burns my throat like a poison. Raquel ordered me to let her go. The letter the lawyer delivered two days ago was her last request. She didn't want to be kept alive by a machine, so she signed her life away.

I'm a widower. My wife is gone and I'm seeking solace from a girl who's too young for me.

"Why do you feel guilty?" she asks,

Snapping my gaze to hers, I meet the pretty dark eyes of Riley. Her name is so fitting, a tomboyish blonde with a smile that eases my pain.

"I'm... I shouldn't be here, yet I can't stop myself from coming every day." It's the truth. I've tried to stay away. To focus on work, on other friends, but none of them understand. Not that she does, but what she does understand is loss. That feeling of having nothing left, and having to go on. People expect you to mourn, but they only want you to do it for a certain time. You're only allowed so many days, that many months. Then you're expected to move on, to smile again, to be happy.

"I've tried to ignore you, but you keep coming back," she informs me cockily.

Chuckling, I sit back and regard her. She told me her psychologist is happy with her progress and I wonder if it's partly because I've given her some sort of will to live. The same way she's given me a reason to smile. To laugh, one that isn't forced or fake.

"If I didn't come back you'd miss me." My words startle us both. Mainly because I feel them, from my mouth down *to my core. I'm in a fucking storm with this girl and she's dragging me into the depths. I need to go to Sins tonight to work out this frustration.*

The BDSM nightclub I frequent is the only place I feel normal. But it's the only place I want to see Riley. I want to tie her up and make her cry. I want to spank her ass, her tits, and her clit. To mark her and make her cry out my name. Every woman I'm with when I go there is not what makes me find pleasure. They don't make me come. It's her pretty face I picture when I'm torturing the willing toys.

Oliver says I'm working out my anger on other women because my wife asked me to let her die. I disagree. I think it's because this little girl sitting on the grass is the reason behind me needing a toy. Someone to play with because deep down, I want her. I want to be her Daddy, to care for her, make her happy, but I also want to be her Dominant. A role of the Daddy Dom is unique from others. It's even more intoxicating than I thought. The need to care for her, spoil her with pretty gifts, and to punish her when she's sassy and cocky.

"Perhaps I will miss you," she finally answers. Then she turns her gaze to me. "But, sometimes I wonder if it's because you're a friend, or if I want you to touch me again. Would you *want to do that?"*

"I'll always want to touch you." Brutal honesty. Rough and raspy, my voice gives away a clear indication of what she does to me.

"Good. Let's go inside, a storm is coming." Her words are ominous and she doesn't know how right she is. The darkness that will soon envelop us is not only in the sky, but also in our lives. I have to make a choice soon. I can't do this to her anymore. A forever with me is not something I can offer her, she needs that. To have someone who can be there through it all.

"Mr. Draydon." My name being called drags me from the memory of Riley and how much I wanted her that day. How I wanted to kiss her in the rain and show her men didn't always hurt girls they loved. But I didn't. We walked inside the hospital and I made sure she was safely in her room before leaving for the night. I made a beeline for Sins that night, I had two beautiful girls willing to do anything I wanted, but the only face I saw in my mind's eye was Riley.

Lifting my gaze at the door, I notice the man standing

there with a smirk on his face. I meet the eyes of my new client. I rise and offer a fake smile. "Mr. Fredericks, my apologies, it's been one of those days. Come inside, let's see what we can do for you." As I close my office door, I catch a glimpse of Giana talking to Oliver. Her giggle is enough to set me on edge. Jealousy is new to me, a foreign emotion that seems to take hold every time I'm near her. Or at least, every time she's near my best friend.

Granted, it was my fault for sharing her, but I needed to know how she felt about me. Their friendship seems to have grown over the past month and I wonder if she still wants him. Even though he's started seeing her best friend, I feel an underlying current of desire when she looks at him.

"It's good to meet you, Mr. Draydon, my father couldn't make it today, and since I'm his partner in the business, he's asked me to come in his place. He's been detained in Los Angeles with work. I trust that's not a problem?" The man watches me for a moment, but something about him seems off. I don't like it, but I nod. I'm not sure what it is about this man, but I'll find out soon enough.

"It's no problem at all. Please, have a seat and let's get down to business." Shutting the door, I stroll over to my desk with both my mind and my perception in disarray. Business first, then I'll sort out my little toy.

When my office door flies open three hours later, I glance up to find my little toy staring at me with annoyance. "What's got the panties you're not meant to be wearing in a knot, baby girl?"

She doesn't respond. Instead, she stalks to my desk in her four-inch heels and I'm hard as fuck at her display. Slipping onto my desk, she crosses her legs and pins me with a heated stare. "When were you going to tell me?" Her words drip with anger, which has me furrowing my brows.

"Tell you what exactly, Toy?" My voice takes on a dominant tone, causing a shudder to travel over her delicious body. Scooting back, I cross my arms over my chest and wait for it. The action closes myself off to whatever's coming because if she's found out about the little secret I'm hiding, I'm sure I'm in for the wrath from her pretty pink lips.

"You're on a man hunt for my uncle?" Her voice raises in frustration and her body is shaking with fear. I realize my cover is blown. How am I going to get my balls out of her tight grip now? "I told you what happened to me and you took it on as a personal vendetta. It's not your life to play with here. If you ever find him, he'll know where I am. Why didn't you tell me?" she hisses and I know I have a choice to give her complete honesty, or lie.

However, there has been too many lies between us. Too many secrets and I'm done with them. As much as I want to calm her down, I know she needs to let out the anger before she can accept that I want her.

Her past is filled with too much pain and I promised myself when I was truly ready, I would take her, I would own her, and I would protect her from any harm that comes her way. In that moment, as I watch my beautiful toy, I realize I cannot be one of those men who hurt her in the past. Nothing in our lives is black and white, but there's nothing stopping me from just giving her the truth. Showing her that she can trust me, I reach for her, taking her hands in mine, and I'm grateful when she doesn't pull away.

"Yes, I am looking for him. And you know why? Because I am your Dominant. I'm meant to protect you, keep you safe from monsters. That is exactly what I will do. So, I'd like you to sit the fuck down and let me explain because you storming in here and shouting at me is not something I want to deal with when the whole office can hear us."

I'm inches from her. She's so close I can practically taste her. But before I even get to that, she's going to have to calm herself down. I need to explain, but I also need her to listen calmly, not in the agitated state she's currently in.

"I'm… I want to save you, the same way I did all those years ago," I tell her.

"Save me?" Her words are incredulous. "I didn't need saving."

"No?" I release her hands. Pushing to my feet, I lean in, crowding her with my larger frame. My hands are on either side of her body, pressing into the wood of my desk. I'm barely holding onto restraint, because all I want to do is spank her ass until it's red raw. "And you didn't enjoy it when I came to your room to talk? You didn't seek me out so I could finger your cunt every day?" My questions cause her to flinch. "Answer me!"

"I-I had to." Her confession spills like a poison, seeping into my mind.

"What do you mean you had to?"

Her gaze drops as she sighs. "She asked me to be there for you when she was gone." Her words slam into me with a force so violent it knocks me to my ass in the office chair. Our gazes are locked in confusion and confession.

"What the fuck are you talking about?" My words are an angry growl.

Slipping off the desk, she settles herself in my lap, curling up like I'd just admonished her and she's seeking my approval. "Raquel," she whispers. "She told me to do it, to be yours. Gave me her dying wish that day, telling me that once she's gone you'll be lonely and she didn't want that for you." Her explanation makes no sense. My wife never once spoke of the girl she once pointed out at the hospital. I remember her words so clearly as if she's right beside me murmuring them in my ear.

"You should befriend her. She looks lonely. Perhaps when I'm gone, she can be your new toy."

My wife knew me well. She knew my needs and wants. The thought of her pushing me to a young girl in the hope that I wouldn't be alone when she's gone grips my heart painfully. I'm lost in my confused thoughts when Giana continues. "She would tell me about you. Confess your darkest desires. I told her I wanted them. I wanted to be consumed by a man who would love me. I was her patient since I was ten, until I turned sixteen." It's then that my Toy looks up at me from under her dark lashes with a knowing glare. *Sixteen.* A year before I met her.

Something clicks then and I realize that Giana, or Riley, has always been in my life. A connection that she sought for so long she saw in me. And I recall the day I first saw a ragged little girl. I was at my wife's office. She ran a private psychiatric office in town. I was fucking Raquel on her desk, my hand wrapped around her throat tightly, lost in the pleasure of her body when the door cracked.

I was met with eyes filled with inquisitive awe. I didn't stop, I continued fucking my wife while the girl watched me. I wanted it. I wanted them both on the desk writhing in pleasure. My desires always ran dark, and that day I was dragged into the abyss that was Riley.

The teen watched as I spilled my seed inside my wife. Her lips were parted in shock, a beautiful O. I shut my eyes and allowed Raquel's whimpers to bathe me in their purity. When I opened my eyes again, the girl had gone. She couldn't have been more than fifteen or sixteen. But it was her innocence in the way she watched my animalistic behavior that made me need more. From that day, Raquel and I would go to Sins and have voyeurs watching us. I came harder than I ever had before.

"You were at the door that day," I mumble, furrowing my brows at her.

She nods slowly, trailing her finger down the buttons of my shirt. "I was. I watched you fuck her, and even at sixteen I knew I wanted you. My body responded to you. Then I found out she was taken to hospital not long after that day and I went to visit her. She told me you had a complex for saving innocent girls. That I... I would be your weakness."

"She knew me very well. Always did." The realization dawns on me. My wife planned my future without me knowing. She sent me a girl she knew needed what only I could deliver, but what she didn't know was the road of depravity I would delve into once she died. Giana's mind had been broken by her past, but I could heal her. Or would I end up breaking this shattered girl further?

"She did. I told her all my darkest secrets. And she knew that you'd want me because of my troubled past. The one I ran from on a daily basis. She was my therapist for far too long not to realize that somehow, two people never meant to meet, can find solace in each other."

"You're so broken, little Toy."

"I am. I fucked up most of my life. I did things I'm not proud of." Her deep brown eyes meet mine and she smiles wryly. "The only thing that ever meant anything to me was you. After you left me I thought I'd be able to fix myself, but then I was taken. A man walked into my room and explained that he could *help* me. Instead, he didn't only break my mind, he shattered my soul. I had nothing. He kept me in a cage. I was a pet to him, nothing more." Her confession hurts me in ways I can't fathom.

"What?"

"I was owned as he called it by a man who called himself a Master. But he was sadistic. Things he did to me..." she trails off with her words and I know that if she told me anything more, I'd lose my shit and kill someone.

"I've got you now, Giana. Nothing and no one will ever hurt you again. You have to always tell me everything. Honesty is the only way this will work. Okay?" She nods.

"I found you again and I don't want to lose this. To lose you. I'll never be able to survive that. It's strange how when I got the job at the coffee shop just to see you, it changed me. My nightmares didn't come anymore. The memories seemed to ease their torment. I found Sins because I needed what you gave me so long ago, and I was in awe the first time I saw you walk in that night. I made sure that I was in your path every day." Giana shrugs as if it's normal. As if her mind isn't as broken as her words portray.

"Look at me," I order a little too harshly. "I want you in my life. Never be afraid to ask me or tell me anything. Understand?"

I realize I'm repeating myself, but I can't have her disappearing again. This is it. I'm never letting her go again.

SIXTEEN

GIANA

He knows everything. Those golden eyes glisten as he watches me with a narrow stare. Lifting a hand, he reaches for me. "Look at me, baby girl," he coos with affection, which I didn't expect, and I can't help lifting my eyes to meet his.

"Are you going to leave me?" My question is immature. It's childish and I wish I could swallow it back up. But I can't. My insecurities rear their ugly heads each time I think of the past. Perhaps one day it will finally stop and I'll be a normal girl. A woman. But when I'm in Eli's arms, curled in his lap like this, I'm not a woman, I'm his toy. And some may see that as an immature act. They may see me as weak for needing him, but it's not weakness, it's strength that allows me to follow my heart. It's power that I have that binds me to him. We're tethered and I'd have it no other way.

"Why would I do something stupid like that?" he questions, his mouth quirking into a smirk. "I told you, Toy, you're mine now." His hand trails over my thigh, sneaking its way under the skirt I'm wearing. When he reaches the apex between my thighs, I can't stop the mewl that falls from my lips. He strokes my panties, feeling the wet spot he's caused with his expert touch.

"Daddy," I whimper when his index finger slips below the material and teases my bare lips. Easily slipping into my core, he pumps one digit slowly, torturously, in and out.

"Do you want Daddy's cock inside you, Toy?" he growls, his voice is low and husky. Thick and smooth like a malt whiskey.

"Yes." My response is a whimper, which earns me a harsh swat on my ass. His big hands grip the fleshy globes of my ass, squeezing hard.

"Respect, little Toy."

"Yes, Daddy," I murmur, rubbing my hand over the

bulge in his slacks, enjoying the feel of his hardness.

"Tell me, beautiful. Give me those dirty words," he orders adamantly.

"I want your cock in my pussy, Daddy, please?" I beg like I know he loves. Suddenly, I'm lifted off his lap and placed on the desk. People talking right outside his door send a shudder of apprehension and excitement through me.

"Bend over the desk, lift your skirt over your hips, I want to see those pretty holes." Leaning over the dark wooden desktop with my cheek on the cool surface, I reach for the hem of my skirt, tugging it up and over my hips. His fingers hook on the waistband of my panties, pulling them down my trembling thighs. Eli moves with controlled precision, which leaves me aching, nervous, yet turned on like never before. I know he'll never hurt me. I'm sure that as much as he's dying to ravage me like an animal, he's not. Holding onto the restraint of the Dominant I know he is, he moves behind me silently, like a predator.

A soft groan falls from his lips and reaches my ears, as he presses his thick erection against the globes of my ass. As he tugs my hair, pulling my head back, he meets my gaze with a heated stare. "Open your mouth," he commands gruffly. When I obey, and part my lips, he stuffs my panties in my mouth and grins when I regard him in shock. "I need you quiet." A smirk curls his lips, dark, delicious, and so damn sinful my clit pulses.

Watching him over my shoulder, I hear the belt buckle clink and I know I'm in for it now. In one swift thrust, he's inside me, fully seated. Whimpers fall from my lips, but he doesn't relent. His hips slap against the flesh of my ass, big hands grip the cheeks hard, making me moan into the material. He opens me to his gaze, I feel him thicken inside me and it feels as if I'm about to black out from pleasure.

"You're fucking perfect. You've always been." He grunts with each word as he plunges into me. The head of his cock strokes against that perfect spot inside me that has sparks going off behind my lids. My hands fight for purchase on the wooden desk, but the violence he's fucking me with won't allow me to hold on.

I can't answer, I can only give him my soft sounds. The same sounds I know that turn him into a feral animal.

His hand reaches for my long hair, gripping it in a tight fist as he tugs me back. "Arch your body for me, Toy." The words are hissed in a low murmur. "You feel how my cock fucks you?" He knows I'm unable to answer, but he tugs my head when I don't nod. "It's because your cunt is mine. Your pert little ass, that's mine too. And soon, I'll take your heart, I swear to you." His vow has my core pulsing around him, tightening, sucking him into my body where I need him most. "That's it, baby. Milk my dick inside you. Take all my cum deep inside you. Soon you'll have my baby, and then I'll bind you to me forever." His words are final. They cause my heart to slam against my ribcage, thudding so hard I'm sure it's about to fight its way out of my chest. There's no disputing that this man is mine as much as I am his. He wants forever, and I'll give it to him.

Everything he says soothes the aches and agony in my heart and mind. His promise is something I never thought I'd get. As his free hand snakes its way between the cheeks of my ass, his fingers taunt the tight hole.

He no longer asks permission because he owns me. Two fingers slip into the forbidden entrance, scissoring me open, loosening me for his thick cock. "Come for me, baby. Come on Daddy's cock," he orders in a feral grunt in my ear, which sends me into the darkest abyss of euphoria.

My eyes are shut so tight, all I see is white lights. My nails dig into the desk, my toes curl and my body shudders as I drain his cock with my pussy. Before I have time to grasp what's happening, he's pulled out of me and slammed into my ass. My screech is muffled by the material. Suddenly, the door flies open and my eyes snap to Oliver in the doorway smirking at the scene before him.

He shuts us in the office, his back against the wooden door watching me get fucked hard. "Aren't you a pretty sight." His low gravelly tone reminds me of brandy, thick and syrupy. My eyes widen when he pushes his zipper down and takes himself out, stroking the thick angry erection as his gaze zeroes in on Eli taking my ass hard.

"I'm so fucking close, Toy," the grunt from behind me, comes harshly. My body once again tries to leap from the edge, but I need to wait. The order needs to come from Eli. The two men stare at each other as I'm tugged back by my hair once more. "Look at him, Toy. He loves watching you get fucked."

Whimpers, moans, and mewls are all I'm capable of. The depravity and pleasure sate my hunger and a hand finds my clit at that moment. The man before me is smirking sinfully. Dark and filthy. Being watched like this sends me into another wave of pleasure I never knew I could feel. It's wrong, taboo, but so sensual and erotic at the same time.

"Come for us, Giana," Oliver urges. His hand a blur, up and down, stroking, jerking his cock faster. Biting down on the material that's stifling my voice, I cry out as tears stream from my face and both men howl in satisfaction as Eli shoots his release deep in my ass, while Oliver comes all over his fist.

SEVENTEEN

ELIJAH

"It's been a long while since I've felt normal," she says, dragging my attention back to her bed. Her body is slight in that damn gown they've draped over her. "I don't want to be here anymore Eli. Let me go," she pleads once more. Every day she says the same thing.

My selfish nature is the only thing holding on. I can't find it in my heart to walk away and leave her to die alone. "You know it's not going to happen," I tell her, but she doesn't look at me. Instead, her eyes are trained on the window. I don't know what she's looking for, but she no longer gifts me those smiles I fell in love with.

"You need to move on."

Those words sear me. Slicing into my chest, they wound

me every time she voices them. I can't let her see my pain, but all I want to do is tie her to the fucking bed and whip the weakness from her and bring back the woman I've spent the last eight years with.

"Can you get me water?" she asks, turning her head, finally meeting my gaze. I nod, pushing off the chair, I make my way out into the hallway. There should be water in her room. This is ridiculous. As soon as I reach the nurses station, I find her. The girl I've been speaking to for months.

"Hello," I say to her. Those beautiful eyes peek up at me, and she smiles. She gives me something my wife will no longer offer.

"Hi. Are you here every day?"

"I am," I respond, turning to the nurse, I request a jug of fresh water with lemon. She disappears down the hall informing me to wait for her. Turning back to my little friend, I take in the bruises on her slender wrist. "What's that?" I ask, gesturing to her arm with my chin.

"Nothing," she responds too quickly.

"I know when people lie. Tell me what happened?"

She shrugs, tugging the sleeve of her jacket down to cover the blue and purple marks.

"Life doesn't afford everyone happy times. Some people's lives are filled with dark and dreary moments. I'm sick," she tells me almost proudly. Her smile is innocent, but there's something else hidden beneath her exterior. "The doctor says I've got a dependency. He called it that anyway. He says I latch on to people too easily."

"And when they leave?" I know the answer. I see it in her eyes before she tells me.

"Then I'm alone." Her answer is only half truth. She hurts herself. The bruise is self-inflicted. Before I can say anything more, she turns to leave, but something tugs inside me and I grab her arm.

"You'll never be alone again," I whisper. I don't know where the words come from, but I say them anyway. I don't know how I'm going to keep my promise to her, but I find that I want to.

The moonlight shines silver in the darkened sky. I can't sleep. I can't think about anything other than having Giana by my side. Her body was so responsive, so fucking needy. After her confession, I was stripped down to my soul. I knew there was a reason she'd appeared in my life, but what she told me rocked the very earth beneath my feet.

It's not been easy losing the one person you were meant to spend your life with. The one person you promised forever to. When she finally closed her eyes, I felt my heart lurch, it was a physical ache that gripped me in its rigid claw.

I didn't know how else to move on. I lost myself in the pain I unleashed on others. On the cold, harsh demeanor I portrayed, but deep down, it was my agony that I wanted to rid myself of. I wanted to give it to someone else to bear. I was a fool. I see it now. All those girls, those women. They all meant nothing, a distraction when I wanted something more. Something real. And she was right in front of me all the time. I was just too afraid to allow my heart to feel again. As much as I loved Raquel, I love Giana as well. There's no longer doubt in my mind. Which means I need to tell her I'm looking for her uncle, as well as the asshole who owned her. I'll make sure both men pay.

Oliver has a lead, and soon I'll be drenched in their blood because I will make them suffer. The anger I feel for them stifles me. I've never been one for violence. But what they did to Gia is something I find appalling, evil, and sadistic, and men like that should be taught a lesson.

A soft moan comes from the bed, and I glance over at the beauty asleep on the black satin sheets. Her face is illuminated by the soft silver light from the moon, causing her to look ethereal. An angel, yet deep down, she's as sinful as a devil.

When she rolls over, her hair fans over the pillow, as if the wind is catching it, making it shimmer. Her curves are hidden by the blanket, but I know every inch of them. All her tiny beauty spots, her sweet smooth flesh, and that incredible cunt that I'm addicted to.

Pushing off the window ledge, I pad into the hallway and down to the kitchen. Everything is bathed in darkness. The same dark that I lived in for so long. The house has been part of my happiness, as well as part of my pain. It's been empty for far too long. Each toy I've brought here has been nothing but sex. Emotion hasn't followed me and I didn't want it. Until her. Until Giana. I know now, I can never live without it again.

When the lights went out in my heart, I allowed my

world to be swallowed in the murky emotion that seemed to compliment my demeanor. I didn't see happiness as a place I belonged, as an emotion that could perhaps allow me to be normal again.

I accepted the depravity I dove into, and I allowed myself to come to terms with the new me. The man who uses women like toys. They were nothing more to me. Only holes to fuck and use.

"You're awake?" Her soft voice comes from behind me. The sweet melodic tone that I've come to need. When I turn to her, I can't help drinking her in with my heated gaze. Her body is wrapped in a black satin sheet. Her hair is messy, her eyes droopy with exhaustion.

"I am." I nod. Moving toward her, I reach for her hips and tug her against me. The heat of her warms me, not only my body, but my heart as well. Her curvy frame molds perfectly to mine. She's always meant to be mine. Even my wife saw it. Somehow, she knew that I'd need someone. "I couldn't sleep, you looked so peaceful I didn't want to wake you so I came in here," I tell her, leaning in to plant a soft kiss on her lips.

"And you sitting watching me sleep for the last

hour was just my imagination?" she quips playfully. Her nature is that of a vixen, a naughty little minx that I want to spank. My grip on her tightens. She stares up at me from under her long dark lashes; those eyes pierce me with love. They break down barriers, they desecrate the walls that have kept me safe all these years, and she burrows herself inside me.

"It was. I'd never do something like that. It's creepy," I joke, watching her eyes glisten with mischief. Lifting the corner of my mouth into a smirk that I know she loves to see on my face, I find myself releasing all the pent-up tension and enjoying my time with her.

"It is creepy, you should get help for that." Her response comes along with a kiss on my stubbly cheek. "And you need to shave," she says.

"I thought you liked the feel of my stubble between your sexy thighs, baby girl," I rasp in her ear. The shudder that shoots through her vibrates through me, causing my cock to harden painfully.

"I do, Daddy," she mewls as I lift her, along with the sheet, and press her against the wall in my kitchen. Her body pinned between me and the cold tiles.

"And what else do you like, my little toy?"

My question earns me a cock-jolting whimper. I roll my hips, pressing my hardness to her core, making sure she feels every inch I have for her.

"Tell me," I order, my tone taking on one of dominance and demand.

"Everything." The one word falls from her plump pink lips as a confession. A truth, honest and raw, filled with emotion so heartfelt, I know I have to tell her everything. I need to come clean about finding the monsters that have plagued her for so long. "I love everything about you, about us. Please, just never leave me."

Her plea doesn't only cause me to want her right here and now, it also makes my heart lurch with knowing. I'm in love with this woman. I've fallen down the abyss and I have no other way of finding my way out. I don't want to. She's never leaving my side again.

"I'm not walking away from this, you've got me. All of me. More than anyone ever had. Even…" My words trail off as I can't bring myself to mention my wife's name. Deceased wife. The woman who's no longer here.

The same woman who sent this sweet girl to me.

"I know. It's okay to love two people you know," Gia tells me sweetly, her fingertips trailing my face, her eyes looking at every inch of mine, as if she's trying to see into the depths of my depraved soul. The darkened heart that's been hidden for far too long.

"I'm not used to love." My voice is husky, scraping the truth against my throat, causing it to burn. I don't want to cry, to allow myself to hurt anymore. I've spent years mourning. I've allowed time to race away from me. Not wanting to face each day is not the way to live. I know Raquel wouldn't have wanted that for me. Hell, she even sent someone to be there for me when she was gone. Her heart knew no bounds. For a woman to give her husband to another is something so selfless. She sacrificed her heart by loving me so much that she was willing to allow me to move on while she was lying in a hospital bed dying. The thought of that is mind-boggling, but it renders me speechless, I have to swallow the lump in my throat just thinking about it.

"Then what are you used to?" she questions, dragging me from the thoughts of the past and pulling me back to the present. I should look to the future now. Gia rolls her hips, her heated pussy pressing against my cock, causing me to groan in pleasure. Everything she does makes me needy. Her smile, her words, and especially her body. But it's her mind that seems to call to me. Her soul, that piece of her that she has never given freely to anyone, I know she's offering it to me on a silver platter. I am lucky. I'm beyond lucky. She's perfect. My toy.

"I'm used to hurting girls like you. Taking them and making them cry while I drive deep inside their tight little holes." I grunt out as she continues to rub herself on me.

"Then make me your Toy. Only yours. I'll do anything you want." Her confidence shines through those incredibly beautiful eyes. She wants this so much. So do I. Images of what I want to do to her flit through my mind like a film reel. All the ways I can taunt her, tease her, and bend her to my will. All the while delivering pleasure on her body that she'll never receive from anyone else. I want to take her to subspace. I want to give her the ultimate of pleasures, the only place that a submissive can truly let go. I know she trusts me enough to allow me to do it. And when she finally reaches it, she'll know the true meaning of being with me.

"You think you can handle all of me?" I ask, tipping my head to the side. My eyes narrow as I regard her. I in turn press my cock against her heat. She's already soaked through the sweatpants I'm wearing. Her cunt is delectable, I can smell her sweet arousal as she continues to rub against me. A horny little toy. A kitten that needs to be pleasured until she's screaming so loudly, my neighbors will know who I am and what I can do.

"I can handle all of you and more. You and Oliver. Anything you throw at me, I'll take and I'll accept. If it means being yours." She's confident. I know she'll obey anything I ask of her. I don't want to share her again. As much as I know Oli would love it, this is my time with her. To learn who she is, what she loves, and how her body responds to the different implements I have hidden in the array of cabinets. This time, she cups my face in her hands, pulling me closer to her so our lips touch. The moment lingers sweetly, almost too much so.

I want to pull away, but I can't. There's no way I

can break this connection with her. Something shifts between us then. Something deep. Profound almost. I can't place my finger on it, but I feel it.

"This is love," she tells me. Then her lips open and she licks the seam of my mouth, asking for entry, and I give it to her. Our tongues tangle in a furious dance of passion, need, and desire.

Lust has woven itself around us. A sweet, decadent emotion, dirty and dark, yet so passionate and profound. She's taken the venom that seeped into every part of my life, and turned it into love. When she pulls away, her gaze locks on mine.

"This is lust," she whispers gently. Her words are fuel, dripping onto my cold heart. As if a match has been lit, it burns, slow and steady. A kindling, which trickles through my veins and I find myself alight with need.

"Take me. Right here and now. Hard, furious, and violently," she says, meeting my blazing stare. Her lips part on a moan when I trail the tip of my tongue down her neck, from the back of her ear, finding her collarbone, nipping at it with my teeth.

"Drop the sheet," I growl into her neck, nuzzling

myself in the crook, needing to inhale her, to take her into my veins, into my bloodstream like an addict craving his next fix. As soon as the silk pools on the floor in a black puddle, I shove my sweatpants down and nudge her core. "You ready for me, Toy?"

"Please!"

With one long brutal thrust, I'm buried to the hilt inside her. The slickness of her body takes me in all the way as she cries out my name. Her nails dig into my shoulders as I pull out and drive back in. Fucking her brutally. Molding her body for my cock only.

Her mewls echo around me in a chorus of satisfaction, of pleasure.

"Mine. Mine. Mine." I chant.

It's a prayer for salvation. It's a plea for acceptance. It's an appeal for forgiveness.

"I'm going to hurt you," I utter through clenched teeth. I can't hold back anymore. I need to claim her. I need to own every inch of her. To make her take all of me. To feel her blood bathe me in its purity. I want it. I hunger for it. My lust takes over as I thrust into her tight body.

"Do it." Two words shove me over the edge and I pull out of her, allowing her back on her feet, I spin her around. Her back against my chest. Gripping her hair in my fist, I tug her head back until her neck is obscenely stretched.

Kicking her legs apart, I fuck myself back into her. Her scream is otherworldly. It's primal, basal, just like the need that's fueling me. Her fingers claw at the wall. "Fight me. Fucking fight this," I grunt with each word, and every thrust. She does. She tries to shove away from me, but I'm too strong. I overpower her each time, taking her in an animalistic way.

Reaching for her clit, I tug it harshly, causing her to whimper and cry out again.

"Come for me, Toy," I order as I feel my own release skittering down my spine with white hot speed. Her body pulses, tightens, milking my dick. "That's it. Take it all," I growl, empting my seed inside her tight little cunt.

EIGHTEEN

GIANA

He used me thoroughly this morning. It wasn't a scene. I felt his pain, as he delivered it to me. Somehow, from the moment he plunged inside me, I forgave my past. I let it go and I gave everything to him. He knows my truth. He didn't let me go when I confessed that his wife was the reason I'd found him.

I know now that love between us was and is inevitable. I love him and this morning, I felt a shift between us when he took me. I felt love. It became something so real, a tangible force between us. I'd never seen him so torn, broken, yet filled with desire. When I first met him, he was so much more than just some stranger, we'd gotten to the root of who the other person was. It wasn't just sex, we'd built a friendship over that year. Even though we were intimate, we'd still had our friendship.

When we'd first met, there was always a sexual undercurrent, and when we finally explored it, I never realized the man who'd touched me so intimately could become a beast. A wild animal that let loose on my body. The ache between my legs is present as I move around the office. And every time I feel the twinge, I can't help smiling. I accepted his beast, as he accepted my past. My tormented history that I cannot change has made me who I am today. A strong, independent, yet submissive woman. And Elijah loves that about me. Which only makes me happier than I have been in years.

Over the past few weeks, each day we spend together he slowly batters down my defenses. He breaks down the walls that hide my secrets, and with each discovery, he only offers me more love than he did before.

But it's when we're Dom and sub that the dynamic once again changes. I become another version of me. Like I was always meant to be his. Owned. He opened something I don't think i'll ever be able to hide again.

Not that I want to. I know he wants more from me. More about the man who owned me and hurt me. Even though he's not forced me to tell him, I know deep down he's biding his time. He's intelligent, calculated, so I know it will come up soon. And I need to be ready. I have to be able to come to terms with my past and allow Elijah to mend me in the only way he can. With his love and affection.

For years I believed that I was nothing. William convinced me I was merely a whore to be used as he saw fit. In his anger, he made me believe with each swat, every sting of the whip, and every backhand he delivered, that I was only made to be abused.

I saw emotion in his eyes each night he walked into the basement and unlocked my cage. It was a filthy desire that swirled in his black eyes.

Vile. Disgusting.

Lust. This sinful, yet addictive emotion is what drove him to do what he wanted. Sometimes it forces people to do some of the most heinous things. That's why it's named as one of the seven deadly sins. It wraps you in its warmth, taunts you with its promises. However, deep down you know that as soon as you no longer have it, you'll be left shattered on the floor needing your next fix.

A junkie. An addict.

When Elijah's wife asked me to find him once she was gone, I agreed, but not because I thought we'd be together. Granted, I desired him more than any person I'd been with, but it was the way he looked at me, he pierced me with his gaze. It was intense. As if he could see my wounded soul, my broken heart, and my fragmented mind. He saw me. The only person I'd ever met to be able to look right through me.

Since I was young I'd suffered. Self-harm became more dangerous the older I got because I took more chances. I cut more. I hurt myself in ways that nobody could see. My problems lie rooted in the past. After my uncle, the one man I trusted took advantage of my love, I didn't believe that I was worth anything.

I'll never be good enough.

The words still ring in my ears. The memories of what he did to me. What he told me every day for six months when he'd come into my room. My parents believed he was tutoring me in my school work. I couldn't confess what was happening. Fear overrode my need to survive. So I allowed it to happen.

When I turned sixteen, I couldn't bear it anymore, so I did the only thing I could think of, I took a blade to my wrists and I sliced my flesh. I watched it bleed. The crimson life force dripped from me. Trickling from the porcelain skin that made me so *pretty* as he called me. I no longer wanted to be pretty. I wanted to make the pain end.

The doctors didn't know what to do with me anymore. Since I was ten, I'd suffered from something. They diagnosed me with ADHD, then when I turned thirteen they decided it was something else. Depression. What normal teenager gets depressed?

I giggled when they told me. It was funny to know that there was a name to my problem. My mind played with me, it toyed with my emotions. When I met my reflection in the mirror, I didn't see a child, I saw a broken toy. A doll that needed fixing, but would never find that missing part.

It hurts. It tears you apart. Something you'll never be able to come back from. Now, when I look at Elijah, I know he is my missing piece. Perhaps I wasn't meant to be the beginning of his story, but I'm supposed to be the end. We've both been through hell, and we've come out on the other side only to find each other again.

I've never been lucky. It seemed to evade me, but this time, it feels as if I've finally hit the jackpot and I've won. When he walked into my room that first time, I knew that I would become attached. A seventeen-year-old girl, needy for a man who's almost twice her age. But I wanted it. I was like a drug addict, needy and wasted on him. He got me high on his touch, his words, his kiss. And even now, I want only him.

As soon as I kneeled for Eli, submitting to him, I knew what I was meant to do. I found my strength. I found my confidence. Because as much as he thinks he's in control, I'm the one with all the power. I choose to submit. To give him what he needs. The ache to please him runs deep in my bones. To the very marrow of who I am.

The moment William walked into my room, and I believed Eli had left me, I thought William would be the man to own me and I would willingly submit to him.

But when I realized what a monster he was, I realized it wasn't what I wanted. I thought I was a bad submissive. He told me enough times that I was. Instead, it was because I wasn't meant for him. He found pleasure in torturing me rather that caring for me. My well-being was nothing to him. With Elijah, it's different.

"Are you leaving early today?" My colleague, Mira, glances at me. She's new to the office. When she started two weeks ago working for Oliver, I noticed there was an electric current between the two, and I have a feeling she does more than answer his calls when he's in meetings.

He's been well-behaved around me, but I know it's only because Eli has probably warned him off. He shared me once. It was the first test I'd passed. Giving in to my Dominant's demands. Allowing my heart and mind to trust him, I gave him my submission that night. And I don't regret a moment of it.

I nod and smile. "Yes, I'll be back in an hour." I make sure my calls are forwarding to the reception desk, my calendar is blocked out, and I know that Eli isn't coming back to the office today. I told him I'm meeting a friend for coffee, I hope that he doesn't question me, because I can't lie to him about where I'm really going. One more meeting and this will be over. I can finally come clean and explain what I've been doing.

Grabbing my purse, I wave a quick goodbye to Mira and head out of the building. The bustle on the street is enough for me to get lost in. If by some chance one of Eli's friends sees me, they won't recognize me walking into the doctor's rooms.

Carrick and Mason live close by, and for them to see me would only lead to questions. They'll then ask Elijah what's wrong, which would only make matters worse. So, I duck my head, and speed walk in the heels he asked me to wear this morning, hastening my way through the lunch time crowd.

My phone vibrates and I pull it from my purse, finding Eli's name glaring at me. Accusing me of lying to him. Of not telling him where I was really going this afternoon. *I need to confess.* But I need one more session. Just this one and I can put the past behind me. Even my doctor said I'm healthy again. That there isn't any more risk of me falling into old habits.

His message is sweet. He misses me. Since I started

working for him full time, I've been surprised at how professional he's been. A small kiss on the cheek, or a smile here and there, but nothing more. It's only in private he really allows himself to become unrestrained.

Yes, we've played in his office after hours. And one or two lunch hours. But that's it. The only other time besides that, is when I'm in his house, kneeling, waiting, and naked. I have a feeling he'll ask me to move in. And I know I'll say yes. To everything he's offering. I want him. To be his partner, his submissive, his Toy.

Before I walk into the offices of my doctor, I tap out a quick reply. *See you later.* And I add a kiss at the end. Stepping into the air-conditioned room, I smile at the receptionist who glances up to greet me.

"I'm here for my two o'clock," I tell her with a smile.

"Yes, Giana. Take a seat and he'll be with you in a moment." She continues tapping at the computer when I only offer a nod in response. Flopping into the plush velvet seat, I turn my phone off, and sit back. My schedule is routine now. Work, sleep, fuck, and therapy. I wanted to stop the sessions, but when I spoke to Dr. Harrow, he said he'd like to do one final hour with me before he signs me off.

There haven't been any nightmares in weeks. Months even. I'm done taking medication. I'm finished with seeing a psychotherapist because I am in control, and I no longer need to be babied. I'm a grown woman.

"Gia," the deep rumble of Dr. Harrow comes from my left. When I open my eyes, I take in the six-foot-something hulk of a man. He's handsome, with deep green eyes and black-rimmed spectacles. He doesn't wait, instead, he walks into the room, and when I join him, I shut the door with a resounding click.

Settling myself on the usual chair, which overlooks the harbor, I inhale a deep breath as he seats himself opposite me. It's silent for a long while before I glance at him and take in how he's watching me, as if I'm the most intriguing thing in the room. Perhaps as a patient I am. He's probably trying to see if he can work out if I'm healthy or not. After a lifetime of sitting in rooms like these, I'm used to it. The unnerving feeling no longer taunts me.

"So," he starts. "Tell me what's happening. Do you still have the nightmares?"

I don't have to think about it because I've been free for so long, I don't even recall when the last time I had a nightmare was. Since I've been with Eli, I haven't dreamt about those times when he walked out the first time.

When I escaped the dungeon, I had them every moment I closed my eyes. I couldn't blink without the horrors staring back at me. Now, I'm no longer a prisoner to my own mind. "No," I answer honestly. "It's been over two months."

"That's a turn around. And what do you think has eased them off? I know you're not taking your medication I prescribed." He admonishes me like an errant child. The pills make me sick, sleepy, and depressed. More so than I already was.

"I've…" My voice trails into silence. *Do I tell him about Elijah? Will he need to know the details about my sex life?* Yes. He needs to know everything, but I find myself holding back. I don't want to tell him.

"You need to be honest with me for this to work, Gia," he warns. When I lift my gaze to him again, I nod. I understand. Life is about honesty. My past is littered with too many lies and people trying to hurt me.

"I've been seeing someone," I confess. He nods, but doesn't say anything. He makes notes on the page before him and then meets my gaze.

"Tell me about him," he asks, and I do. I give him everything. The way we met, when, how, and why. Honesty. It falls from me like a waterfall, and I feel lighter when I finally finish my story.

He's silent for a long while as he shakes his head. I know he's disappointed in my answer. This isn't the treatment he wanted for me. He knows about my past with William and submitting to another man is not the best idea. But what he doesn't understand is that this is different. This is a real relationship.

"He's good for me. I've been stronger for a while. Before him. It's been—"

"I'm happy for you. It's perhaps what you needed all along. I must admit, I'm not entirely happy you're putting so much pressure on this relationship, but…" He trails off with his words, then meets my gaze. "I believe you'll be able to move on. To live without a session in here. However." He lifts his pen, pointing it at me as if I'm a child who's getting a scolding. "If those memories, those nightmares ever return, you call me. I want to know."

I'm stronger now. More so than I've ever been. There is no way I'm going to allow myself to go back to what I used to be. To hurt myself. He waits for me to respond, his eyes resting on me almost affectionately.

"I will. Thank you."

"I believe you're a much stronger woman than you used to be. When you first walked in here, I didn't believe you'd be able to live a normal life, but it seems you've proved me wrong." He smiles then. A soft, gentle one.

"I've tried hard to live a normal life. It's all I've ever wanted. Love, family, just someone to go home to." He nods in understanding. He has all my old files. Pages of notes from my previous doctors. All my problems. Those things I long believed I was.

"You'll have it. Now go home to Elijah and tell him everything. Remember, Giana, honesty is the only way to continue being as strong as you are."

"I know," I respond, pushing up, I grab my purse and offer him my hand to shake. "Thank you for everything.

I'm not sure I'd be here without you."

"Oh, I doubt that. You were always on the road to recovery, I think it was this Elijah who was the one to finally make sure you stuck on that road."

With that, I make my way out of the office for the last time. My head held high and my heart soaring with happiness. Tonight, I'll tell Eli everything. I'll recall all I went through, and I'll curl myself in the safety of his arms. The only place I long to be.

NINETEEN

ELIJAH

She's hiding more from me and I want to punish her severely. I want to make her tell me what secrets are sitting on her tongue. But forcing her to tell me more will only scare her and that's not what I want to do. I have to tell her I found her uncle, but the man that owned her is elusive. Someone that's too clever to be caught easily. However, I'm going to make sure I find him. I'll ensure that Gia's mind is at ease and she'll know she's safe from the past.

"Elijah?" Her voice is tentative behind me, and I turn to find my beautiful toy leaning against the door jamb. She's perfect. Every inch of her is utter perfection. No other woman has gripped me the way she has. She's dressed in a pair of shorts that cause me to grow hard in my slacks, the material hugs her hips, and stops just under her ass offering me a view of her slender, yet toned legs. Almost a look of innocence, if not for the color of lust she wears on her torso. She must've been working out because of the tiny sports bra that cups her breasts, which only serves to send a wave of lust through me.

"Toy, come here," I command, and she obeys. Her bare feet pad over to me in tentative steps. Long lithe legs taunt me from the bottom of her shorts, as she settles on my desk. My home office is the only place I allow work to enter my home. Having her here is still so new to me. She swings her legs like a little girl. Her eyelashes bat playfully and her mouth is pouty, with full lips, and I now find myself rock hard.

"What are you doing?" she questions innocently, but I know there's nothing innocent about this woman. Something's on her mind. She hardly comes into my office, unless I summon her. Unless she's finally going to give me the whole truth.

"I was working, but my mind got distracted. Why are you walking around in your panties?" I ask, tugging on the tiny blue shorts she wears.

"They're yoga shorts. I was working out in the cinema," she informs me.

"Do you want to be my little girl?" I ask.

She nods, pushing her lower lip out in a pout, which only further hardens my dick. Jesus, this woman will be the end of me.

"Yes, Daddy," she mumbles in her sweet voice.

"Take those fucking panties off and sit on my lap." My words are brisk as I order her around. My gaze drinks her in reverently as she slips from the mahogany top and slides the tiny blue panties down her legs. She's bare underneath, gifting me a view of her smooth little cunt.

I love my toys bald, smooth to the touch because when I'm devouring them, I want to taste their essence. I want the roughness of my stubble on those lips, causing friction to turn them into whimpering dolls.

Once she straddles me, I look up at her. Our gazes sear through each other. There's definitely something on her mind, I can see it in her eyes. She's like an open book to me. I can read her effortlessly. That's what I love, knowing her innermost thoughts, fears, and that's what makes a good Dominant. Being able to tell what your submissive is feeling by casting a quick glance in their direction.

"Do you like when Daddy uses your holes?" She nods in response, earning her a swift spank on her pert ass. "Words, Gia."

"Yes, Daddy," she pouts. Her face turning almost petulant and I hold back the urge to chuckle.

"Good girl. Rub your cunt on my crotch." Her hips roll at my order, causing me to groan in pleasure. Her heat is addictive. Her body moves over me and I grip her hips to hold her still. I'm dying to fuck her, to fill her with my release, but I need time to properly show her she can trust me.

"Daddy," she whines, earning her another spank.

"I want you to sit on the desk. Spread your legs as wide as they will go." She moves swiftly. Her body is quickly perched on my desk and her heels are up on the top, with those beautiful thighs open lewdly to my hungry gaze.

I lean in, my chair putting me at the perfect height.

My tongue laps at her pink flesh. Her arousal drips like honey onto my tongue, my chin, and I savor it. Lifting my gaze, I meet her lust-filled one and offer a smirk before I dip my tongue into her core.

She cries out profanities, which only makes me lick her faster. Taking two fingers, I slide into her, crooking them against the soft spot which has her begging for more, for an orgasm, but I shake my head. With my fingers fucking her, I reach down with my free hand and pull out my cock, fisting it in sync with the way I move inside her.

"Please, please, Daddy," she pleads, her voice driving me insane, her body bucking against my face. Tonight, she'll give me all. As I will offer her the truth. There's something more I need to do, but before I can, we need to lay our cards on the table. I'm not leaving her, no matter what she tells me.

I feel her cunt pulse around my digits and I pull them from her immediately. "Be a good girl and breathe," I tell her. Making sure she's almost relaxed, I rise and slap my cock on her clit. The movement making her curse me, only earning her a chuckle.

"Please," she asks, looking at me with a teary gaze.

"Tell me. I want to know what you're hiding," I say, slipping the crown of my cock up and down her drenched slit. "I need to know why you're not being honest with me." My words are low, husky. I taunt her with the tip of my shaft, slipping it in a small inch before pulling out again.

"I don't know what—"

Without waiting for her to continue, I slam into her hole, causing her to scream my name. I pull out again, knowing she's needy, I smile as she bares her teeth at me. Once again, I taunt her clit by spanking it with my hand this time, making her scream. Her head drops back, and I know she's teetering on the edge. Just where I want her.

"Please—"

"Tell me, Gia," I order, offering another harsh swat on her clit, making her whole body tremble. She's gripping her ankles so tight I'm sure she'll be bruised. Another swat and another. Her pussy is turning red and my dick is leaking arousal. It needs inside her, but I want answers.

"I'm going to a psychiatrist," she admits finally.

Something I'm not shocked over. I figured after what she'd been through, there would be need for specialist help.

"Why?" I ask, slapping her clit once more. Her thighs shudder, her hands are clawing at my desk now, and her hips are bucking up toward me, but I don't allow her to take pleasure.

"I've had nightmares, since I was a teenager. They come in spurts," she rattles off quickly. "I… He says it's my fear of being alone. My… I can't be alone," her confession is mumbled, but I hear every word. Even the one's she doesn't say. And my heart drops to my stomach. It's not some childish fear, it's deep rooted. Her pain is mine. I feel it down to the marrow in my bones.

Guilt weighs on me then and I gently connect us. Her body accepts me into its heated depths. Once I'm fully seated, I lock my gaze on hers. "Do not ever be afraid again, I'm never leaving you. Do you understand me?" She has nothing more to fear because I'm here now and I will not walk away from her. I don't think I have the ability to.

I don't move. She doesn't shift. It's as if time stopped

and the only two people who can make it come alive again is us. My toy and me. She and her Daddy. I've always thought of myself as a loner, but with her in my life, I know I'm where I belong. I'm hers.

Losing the love of my life caused me to push everyone away, I didn't want to say those words to anyone again. The women I fucked were merely holes for pleasure. Nothing more. But now, looking at Gia makes me realize I can say it again and there's nothing wrong with feeling it again.

"I love you, Gia." The truth tumbles free. She watches me for a moment, her breath catching in her throat and her tight little pussy pulsing around my shaft. I'm hard. Rock fucking solid. I move then, it's slow, sensual. This is not us fucking, this is not a Dom and his sub. This is a man and a woman who love each other.

When she smiles, my heart thuds, banging against my chest. She doesn't utter the words back to me, but I know what she needs. Time. My hips move then. My pace is torturous. Slow and methodical. Back and forth. In and out. I'm hers. All hers.

I've laid my cards out on the table, now it's her turn.

She claws at my back and I reach for her legs, wrapping them around my waist. I lift her from the desk and shift to the wall, pressing her against the dark paint. Her creamy skin is such a contrast to her dark hair and the concrete behind her.

No words. Only actions. I slam into her. I fuck her. Pulling out, and driving back in, I hit her deep, knocking the breath from her as I take her. My hands grip her ass, squeezing hard until she's crying out. I know she needs this. It's her outlet.

Her nails dig into the skin on my shoulders and I'm sure she's drawing blood, but I don't care. I shift my hand closer to the ring of muscle that I want to fuck violently and slip a finger into her. No lube. No preparation. Her eyes snap open and her mouth drops wide in a cry that is wretched from her core.

"Daddy," she hisses as I fuck both her holes. "I need… I want…"

"Come on my fucking dick, Toy," I grunt. My mouth finds purchase on her neck, my teeth biting down hard, causing her to pulse around me. Her body flutters with her orgasm, which milks my own release from my balls, and I empty myself inside her.

We're silent in our euphoria. Connected in our pleasure. And brutal in our love.

I know she loves me. I see it when she looks at me. I've only ever seen one other woman look at me like that. And she's dead. It's time to move on. Time to love again. It's in that moment I finally say goodbye to Raquel. Not only goodbye, but *thank you.* If it weren't for her selfless behavior, I wouldn't be here today.

"I love you, Eli." Gia's words settle around my heart. I don't look at her. I can't. Not right now because she doesn't know that the thought that's racing through my mind in that moment will change both our lives.

Tears, thick and heavy fall from my eyes and I keep my toy close. I hold her like she's my lifeline in a rough sea. She's the one who will keep me from the darkness and I'll be the one to hold her above the depths. We anchor each other. And if either of us walks away, the other won't survive.

Leaving a note on the pillow beside her, I can't help grinning because I know it's going to leave her aching for more. That's the idea. As much as I'm an asshole to her, I'm so in love with this woman, I want only the best for her. I want to care for her. Look after her. She's my responsibility and no other man will gift her what I do.

Walking through the house, I take in the space. As much as I love this house, I know it's not a home. I want to give Gia that. But before we can even get there, I want to know what that asshole did to her. I wanted to talk through it with her last night, but after confessing our love, I didn't want to taint that with the vile recollections I know haunt her.

We can work together. We can heal together. Like a couple should. I want to know her mind, every dark corner of it, and when I learn the truth, I'll shed light on her life. On her present, and on our future.

Grabbing my briefcase, keys, and wallet, I turn to head out to the garage. My mind is on her. It's been on her since the moment I first laid eyes on her. Somehow, as fucked up as it sounds, I know my wife sent her to me for a reason. For me to move on. And I've finally done it. But there's one thing I need to do before I can give myself to Gia fully. It's my final farewell. It's time to go back, in order to move forward. So, I've planned the morning to let go of the past, to thank my wife for what she did, and to look to my future with the woman that's stolen my heart right from under me.

One thing I've been putting off for years, I must now face. It's time. I need to do it. So, I get in the car and start the engine. The purr is enough to calm me for now. As the sun rises on the horizon, I see it as a fresh start. A new day. Smiling, I pull out onto the road and make my way to the place I haven't visited since I laid Raquel to rest in the ground. I go now, to say goodbye.

TWENTY

GIANA

The sun streaming through the window warms me as I open my eyes to a new day. A smile curls my lips. My heart is light, free. I feel love cocoon me like never before. Last night when Elijah confessed he loved me, I didn't respond immediately. I couldn't. Not because I don't, but because I was choked up with emotion so profound, words didn't come to me.

Rolling over in bed, I reach for Eli, but he's already left and I find the sheets cold. For the first time in a long while, I know he'll be back and I don't for once doubt it. My hand finds a folded card on his pillow, and when I open it, my eyes devour the words eagerly.

Gia,

Last night was profound. It wasn't something I take lightly. Uttering those words, confessing my love for you is no easy feat. I've not loved in a long time. I didn't think I would again. I didn't know if my heart would ever beat again, but you my sweet have brought it back to life.

Each moment with you is different. It's new. Refreshing. Something I need and want. We will heal each other. There is no easy path to find happiness, but I'm willing to walk it with you. I want us to entwine our lives together.

I can't stop thinking about how much I want to inch into your body with every thrust of my hips against yours. I want to take you into the darkness alongside me. Gia, I ache for you to stand on the very precipice of forever, of love, and find me beside you, holding your hand.

Nothing else that's happened between us matters. The past is just that. This morning, I've gone to do something I've needed to do for a long time. I'm finally letting go of the history I shared with someone else, in the hope that I can look to the future with you. Look to what we have now, and build that into something both of us need and want.

The only thing I need is to feel you ride me through one

violent orgasm after the next. The orgasms I give you. No other man. I will no longer share you. I can't. You're now in my heart, you're embedded in my mind, and deep down, you know that my soul is yours. You're mine.

I want to feel your beautiful body crashing into mine like waves on the shore. I want to take full possession of you, to collar, leash, and claim you. Taking total ownership of your mind, body, and cunt. I want to lap at you for hours and feel your nectar drip, trickle, gush onto my tongue, my lips, my face.

I want the sweet poison of your release in my veins as I am in yours.

Now that you're thinking of all the ways I'll take you, I know you're wet. Drenched for me. Stay that way. Do not touch yourself. Not even once. You'll be mine tonight.

Eli

I smile, thinking about how my life has turned out. Spending years in hospitals, therapy sessions, and here I am. With a man who loves me. We may not have had the easiest start, but deep down I feel as if our forever will be happy. I never planned a future. Even when I was little,

I didn't think I'd ever have a family of my own, a white picket fence and a husband. Even if Eli and I never get married, if we just stay Dom and sub, I'll know he loves me. He's given me his heart as I've given him mine.

Children flit into my mind then. I close my eyes and envision two little boys. Spitting images of Elijah. I'd like that and I find myself holding my stomach, rubbing small circles over it. I've been on the pill for as long as I can remember, and perhaps, now that we're in a good place, I can talk to him about trying. The thought stutters my heart and I can't help a lone tear of happiness trickling from my eye.

Pushing off the bed, I head to the kitchen with my mind on a family, two children and a man who will grow old with me. I set my phone down and pad over to the coffee machine.

Once it's heating up, I grab eggs from the fridge, and pop bread into the toaster. Since Eli isn't at work, and Oliver has Mira, I can take my time getting ready this morning. There aren't any meetings, and if calls come through, I know Mira can handle it.

The bread pops from the toaster and I prepare

breakfast with a smile on my face. My phone buzzing from the countertop startles me, thinking it's Eli, I swipe the screen, not looking before greeting the caller.

"Hello, handsome." I smile into the phone hoping to hear his thick, husky rumble.

"I'm never far away, little one." The voice that greets me instead is like ice over the warmth that Eli left in my heart. "Did you think running away and giving your slutty little body to someone else is acceptable? It's not love, it's lust."

"I walked out. This is over. I'm no longer yours, William." My voice trembles with fear at the memories of what he did to me. The images in my mind are violent, turbulent, but I force them away.

"You can never leave me, whore. I paid for you. Do you remember that? Does he even know what you are? A paid fucking whore. Watch out, I'll come for what's mine. You."

The line dies leaving me in a cloud of terror. Eli can't find out about what happened to me with this monster because he'll want to hurt William, and I'm afraid that Elijah will be the one hurt. I don't want him to know what horrors I faced. How broken I was when he left because guilt will weigh heavily on him. I ran, I fled, and even with Carrick's help, I haven't truly gotten away. Instead of escaping the monster, I've just been playing his game.

Rage simmers in my blood. My fight or flight instinct tells me to run, to leave Elijah and allow him to find someone better. Deep down I know I won't. Wrath, anger, revenge spur me on and I hit dial on Carrick's number.

"Gia," he says, his English accent thick and heavy with sleep and I realize it's early in the morning. "What's wrong?" I hear him shuffling and I wonder if I'd disturbed him with one of his submissives.

"I... Carrick, I need your help. It's life or death," I utter the words ominously.

"Tell me where you are. I'll come to you," he responds. His voice sounds alarmed by my call, and I know he's the only one who can help me out of this. There are secrets that Carrick holds about his past and about what he's capable of that makes me sure he'll be the only one who can take William down without being killed. The man who's coming for me is dangerous, not only to me, but to anyone who stands in his way.

"I'm at Eli's house. Can I come to you instead?" I question, worrying my lip at the thought of having him here and Elijah walking in to me confessing my darkest secret. I'm already up the stairs and shoving off my panties and tank top while trying to listen to Carrick on the other end of the line.

"Yes, I'll have the car pick you up in twenty minutes."

"Thank you," I sigh, relieved.

Once I hang up, I take five long deep breaths. Anxiety is tight in my stomach, coiling like a serpent ready to strike. I need to keep calm. I need to be in control if I'm going to survive this. Grabbing a change of clothes, I pad into the bathroom and turn on the shower. Before the water has warmed up I'm under the spray, holding back tears at the thoughts of what's going to happen. If *he* does come for me, I don't think I'll survive the aftermath.

"Please," I beg, whispering to no one in particular. "Please, let this work out." Moments later I turn off the taps and step out of the shower with my stomach rolling with fear and my heart thudding in my chest. The flurry of butterflies that Eli left have disappeared and in their place an eclipse of moths is now swarming within me.

Once I'm dressed, I pull my hair into a messy bun and race back to the living room where my keys and purse are lying on the counter top. *It's going to be okay. You're in control. You're safe.* The chant in my head repeats like a chorus. I head out to the front door. Pulling it open, I find a small black box waiting for me on the welcome mat. With shaky fingers, I lift it and snap the lid back. A small white gold diamond necklace sits nestled in the black velvet.

It's beautiful.

Intricate, delicate, and breakable.

I lift it gently only to notice the small pendant that hangs from the chain. A silver disc with one single red diamond, the color of blood. The word *whore* is engraved below the stone. William is playing his mind games with me. He knows why that word hurts me so much. He knows too much. He knows me better than I know myself. The man who was meant to care for me, who was hired to help me, scarred me more than any bruises he left on my skin.

The room is dark. My fear turns my stomach tight. Suddenly, the fire blazes. Flames lick the wall rising up to the chimney. He promised he'd be gentle tonight. But I know better. I know the man I've been forced to kneel for is a monster.

He wreaks havoc with my mind, my heart, and he breaks my body like I'm glass. Nothing more than a worthless ragdoll. He crouches before me, I feel his eyes burn into me. I don't look. I force myself to never meet his eyes when he's in this mood. And then he speaks.

"Riley, do you know you're nothing to me?" He chuckles harshly. "Nothing, but a worthless whore." He grips my hair, tugging it back, making sure that I'm looking into his sapphire eyes. I'm slumped on my knees, naked, shivering, but it's not because of the cold. It's the terror he elicits in me.

It's how he gets off. Hurting women. He calls himself a Dominant. A sadist. But he's none of those things. What he is, is an abuser.

"Look at the mascara tears, they paint pretty pictures on your face. Lines of sadness because you know how filthy you

really are. Not even your parents wanted you. That's why they sold you to me." Once again, he reminds me of why I'm really here. How the people who are meant to love and care for me, sold me.

His palm strikes my face with a sting so hard it brings tears to my eyes. He rises, shoving his zipper down and pulling out his cock. It's hard already.

"Open your fucking mouth," he sneers. He's not always been like this. It started when I tried to run the first time. My lips part, he doesn't wait but instead, forces his thick erection down my throat. Once. Twice. Three times and I feel my throat constrict. I gag, retch, and then it comes. I puke on the floor and he laughs. "If you do that again, I'll make you lick my fucking asshole, dirty bitch," he grunts as he forces his cock inside my mouth again. The bitter acidic taste still on my tongue as he face fucks me violently.

The sounds echo around me. Around us. The gurgling sound of my choking, his animalistic grunts are like a sadistic song that haunts me.

"All you are," he says in between thrusts. "is a collection of holes. A mouth," thrust "a cunt," thrust "and ass," each drive of his dick goes deeper. "Mine to take as a possession."

My hands come up, trying to push him away, but I know it's no use. There's no point in fighting. He loves it. It turns him on.

"You no longer have a choice," he tells me as he spits in my face. He wretches his cock from my mouth and lifts me onto the table. Bent over, he kicks my legs apart. "I don't want to see your filthy face. I'm going to give it to you like the greedy slut you are." He slams into my ass, forcing his cock so fast causing me to screech in pain. I'm clawing at the table, but I'm helpless.

His body pistons into me. Harder and faster. Pain so acute races through me and I feel the trickle of liquid from my torn ring of muscle down my thighs. Tears are no longer an outlet for me. They burn as they race down my cheeks.

My body slams against the wood. His hips pound against my ass, skin slapping, his hand grips my hair, wrenching my head back. "Don't you come, little bitch. Don't you even dare," he grunts like a rabid dog. "Because, you are my worthless whore. And you'll know that I now own you. All of you. You're my everything. My world."

My whimpers are filled with pain. I want to plead for him to let me go, but I don't. His body jerks, his cock thickens, and he fills me with his hot seed. It burns and stings. Quickly, he pulls out of me and shoves me to my knees.

"Clean it," he commands, thrusting his filthy cock into my mouth making me retch once more. My eyes shut tight as I concentrate on not throwing up. The metallic taste of blood mixed with his release turns my stomach. "Good whore." His hand taps my head as he leaves me on the floor until the next time he needs to violate me.

I shove the box into my bag and head for the steps which take me down to the long driveway. Racing down the cobblestones, I hit the button to open the ornate gates and as they slide open, I see the car with blacked out windows waits for me at the sidewalk and the driver is waiting to escort me to Carrick. Only he can help me.

"Hello," I say, smiling at the man in uniform.

"Ms. Gia," he says, opening the back door for me. I slip into the bench seat and take a deep calming breath. *It's going to be okay. It will be. It has to be.* I pull out my phone and find a message from Rick.

Driver is on his way. Stuck in traffic. Stay indoors.

When I snap my gaze to the driver, a black partition slides up.

"Hey! Hey!" I slam against the glass, but it's too strong. I try kicking at it, but it's no use. When I try the doors, they're locked. Of course, they fucking are. Terror grips me, stealing the breath from my lungs. Quickly, I swipe my screen and hit dial on Carrick's number.

"Baby girl," he answers. His voice coming through hesitant and wary. He should be because I think I'm in a world of shit.

"I'm in the car. A car. He's found me." My words are ominous.

"Fuck, where are you heading? Can you see what's around you? Better yet, turn on your phone's GPS. I'll have my men track you. Stay calm. Do not engage him." He's telling me things I should know. Important things, but they filter from my mind when a scent fills the car. My eyes feel heavy. Too sleepy. When I try breathing, I realize the driver must have emitted something in the back of the car.

"Rick, find me…" It's the last few words I utter

before sleep steals me.

TWENTY ONE

ELIJAH

The cemetery is quiet as I look around and take in the number of memorials and graves. All people who've left families behind, friends, lovers. I bring my gaze back to the headstone with Raquel's name on it. *Beloved Wife.* She was that and so much more.

"I have put off coming here for so long, but it's time, my sweet." I tell her. The warmth of the sun bathes me in its glow. As if she's looking down on me and smiling. She had the most incredible smile. It could light up any room. "I spent years in the dark. When you died, I lost myself. I forgot who I was. There was no longer the strong, courageous Elijah Draydon. All that was left was a shell. I was a widower."

Leaning in, I place the single red rose on the ground beside the headstone. I don't feel pain as I do it. I no longer have an aching heart. That causes me to smile, a small one, but a smile nonetheless.

"You sent Riley to me for a reason. She's all grown up now. A woman. Her name is Giana. I'm still not sure why she changed her name, but as we learn more about each other, I'll find out the rest of her story." Sighing, I glance around, I'm not sure if I'm waiting for an answer from her, a response of some kind, but I don't get one. "I want to marry her, babe. I want to give her a family."

Silence settles around me after I admit what I've been thinking. Each time I make love to her, fuck her, I spill my seed inside her, wanting and needing her to fall pregnant. I want that. The perfect family.

"You were the chapters of my life I'll never forget. I'll re-read those pages to Giana, but I know what you tried to do. Looking after me even when you were gone, you were always so selfless. A submissive even in death. Well, your plan worked. It may have taken a few years, but I'm happy. I'm content. And I've come today to say goodbye. Raquel, I realize I can't move forward if

I'm still holding on to you. It's not fair to Gia. And it's something I need to come to terms with. You're gone. I'll never stop loving you. In some way…" My words trail off as a car passes slowly. I glance at it, then look away.

I look toward the trees in the distance, wishing they'd allow me a glimpse of Raquel, but they don't.

"Goodbye, my sultry Toy. Thank you for the years you gave, and the heart you saved. I'll forever be grateful for you. I love you," I utter the words and turn away. I may come back again someday, bring Gia along with me, but today I needed to do this on my own. I had to let go and know that I'm strong enough to finally lay my wife to rest.

When I reach the car, I press the key fob and slip into the driver's seat. Before I can start the engine, my phone vibrates and I pick it up to find fifteen missed calls and thirty unread messages. Immediately my heart rate spikes. Opening the first message, I find Carrick's name glaring at me.

Get to Sins now. It's life or death

Where the fuck are you, man? Gia is in danger. Get your ass here now

I don't read the rest, instead I dial Rick's number while I start the engine.

"Jesus, Eli. Where the—"

"What happened? I can be at Sins in ten minutes." He sighs and I wonder if he's stalling because he doesn't want to tell me, or if something more serious happened that he can't tell me. "If you don't tell me, I swear to God—"

"Her Dom, the one she escaped has her. He contacted her this morning and..." His words trail off and I'm ready to punch a hole through a fucking brick wall if he doesn't explain himself. "William found her. She called me and I told her I'd have a car pick her up, but when I messaged her to tell her the driver was going to be late, she responded by telling me she was in the car already. She called me, but after a minute of talking, she went offline."

"Her GPS—"

"I've tried. It's been shut off. I can't find her, Eli. I

have men working on it." My foot presses down on the gas, weaving through traffic with my body tense. Anger courses through me. Guilt. I left her alone this morning. I should've taken her with me. This man will pay.

"Find her, Rick," I warn. I'm not angry at him, I know he'll do what's best for my girl, but deep down I'm angry at myself. Hanging up, I focus on the road ahead. All I see is red. I want this monster killed. If I have to spill blood, I'll do it. Fuck the consequences. I've lost her once, I don't intend on doing it again.

I promised to keep her safe. Just last night, I vowed to never let harm come her way and a day after, I'm already breaking that promise. "If you're out there, Raquel, if you can hear me, even for a second, look after her. I'll find her. And when I do, she'll never leave my fucking sight again."

I see the sign for Sins a few hundred meters away and I find myself breathing again. My chest aches, it feels as if someone has punched their way through my chest and they're about to rip my heart right from its cage.

Pulling up to the club, I exit the car without killing the engine and race inside. When I step into the dimly lit space, I find Carrick with at least eight men on computers, phones, all dressed in black suits. They look like they've walked right out of the offices of the CIA.

"Eli," he says, turning to face me as I stalk up to him.

"Have you found her?" He regards me for a moment before shaking his head. "Dammit!" I spin on my heel and slam my fist straight into the glass of the liquor cabinet to my left. The shattering of glass causes the men to stop for a second before continuing their work.

"Eli, I need you calm."

"Calm? Are you fucking kidding me?" I'm roaring, but Carrick doesn't even flinch. He merely watches me for a moment then he nods.

"I get you're worried. I am too. I love that girl, but you slamming your fist into inanimate objects isn't going to help. I have the best men on this job so please, I need you to relax. We will find her, and when we do, she'll need you to be a foundation for her." He's right, so I acknowledge him.

"Fine, but I have to do something."

"At this stage, I have my team working on it. Have

a drink," he says, shoving the bottle of whiskey at me along with a crystal tumbler. I grip the bottle, pouring a triple shot. Slamming the bottle down on the oak counter top, I lift the glass to my lips and swallow the whole shot. It burns, rendering me speechless and emotionless for a moment.

"I need her, Carrick," I tell him, meeting his golden eyes once more. They shine like a predator's, deadly and fierce, and I know that with him on our side, my girl will be saved.

"Elijah, if there was ever a time to trust me, it would be now. I saved her once, and I'll do it again. Even if it's the last thing I do." His brutal honesty eases my fear, but deep down, it makes me wonder why he's never settled with one submissive. If he's so caring, so devoted to keeping girl's safe, something must have happened to have pushed him away from taking on a girl of his own. Someone he could really care for.

He turns and heads to the men at the table, I follow, needing to be a part of this. Even though the alcohol has simmered my rage, deep down there's a volcano brewing and I have a feeling it's going to explode really soon.

"We may have a bite. The GPS on the phone has just been turned on again," one of the men says, pointing at the screen. Both Carrick and I are on our feet, stalking over to the table. I notice the red dot flashing and my heart slams in my chest painfully. She's alive. I'm so sure. I haven't been surer of anything in my life.

The problem is, the spot in question is about two hours away.

"Let's get your girl back. I'll have the private jet fuel up, and wait for us at the hangar." Carrick smirks. Something about this man tells me he'd easily kill someone and not look twice. And right now, that's exactly what I need.

This is going to take too long. We've wasted time standing around, but I know there's nothing more I could've done. I can't help myself, my legs carry me as I start pacing the floor of the club. Sins is a decadent wonderland at night, but in the light of day, it's just a normal bar. There aren't any whips and chains, no sensual women dressed to kill, and no men in suits with roving eyes.

The tension in my shoulders tighten as my mind plays out all the scenarios I'm in for. Thoughts of what my girl is going through loop in my mind and the more they do, the more anger settles in my gut. My blood is boiling by the time Carrick returns from his office.

"Let's go," he says, stalking by me with five men flanking him. I didn't notice it earlier, but they're all armed. I don't ask why or how Rick knows them, I'm just thankful that he does. Because if it weren't for him, I'm not sure I'd be able to do this on my own. Frustration blooms once more when I think about how useless I am to her, to the woman I'm meant to protect.

We reach the car and I join Carrick in the back.

"We'll find her, and don't for one second think this is on you," he tells me as if he could read my inner thoughts. Perhaps he can sense the guilt that's certainly emanating from me. When I meet his gaze, I nod, not knowing what to say to him. "She'll be okay. One thing about Gia is that she's strong. And you'll get her back. I promise," I can't respond because emotion chokes me.

After a long moment of silence, I finally admit it to him.

"I love her."

He looks at me then, a smile on his lips. "I know." He confirms. Perhaps it's evident to everyone else. The car flies through the traffic, not stopping at traffic lights and I'm thankful for that. Each minute that ticks by is a wasted moment where I could be saving Gia.

I'll find you, my sweet Toy. I love you.

TWENTY TWO

GIANA

Thud. Thud. Thud.

One. Two. Three.

My eyes crack open, the throb in my head is blinding, and my body aches. As soon as I shift, I realize I'm naked. My gaze darts around and I know exactly where I am. The stench is so familiar. Too damn familiar.

The recognizable basement taunts me. Cold seeps from the cement walls into my bones. The cage he's locked me in is the same one I spent so many months in. Each day he'd come down here, abuse me and leave. I had no way of defending myself.

I'm not sure how long I've been out, but there's only a sliver of light coming in from the small hole in the wall that used to be my refuge. I'd look to the sky through the small space and pray for death. The cage is big enough for me, and perhaps one more person, but the height forces me to spend my time crouched in the damp. My skin prickles as the cold breeze filters in from the hole close to the ceiling and I can't help shivering so hard my teeth chatter.

There aren't any lights in this place, so as my eyes adjust to the dark, I notice another smaller cage only inches from where I am. "Hello?" I call out, my voice croaky and raspy. There's no sound, no response, just my breathing.

I hear him before he enters the room, so when the rattling of the keys in the door alerts me that he's about to open the door, I crouch down and act like I'm still asleep. I grit my teeth hoping the chattering doesn't alert him that I'm awake and aware of him in the room.

"The little whore is still asleep," he grunts as I hear the clang of metal. Fear skyrockets when I hear a soft whimper and then another loud bang. I don't move. I don't even breathe. He doesn't stay for too long in the room because I hear his voice near the door only moments later. "You're both going to play for me soon," he threatens angrily then slams the door shut. Once again, the keys rattle and I'm unsure of who he was talking to, but I have a feeling I'm going to find out soon enough.

When I shift along the floor of the cage, a gasp comes from my left. I open my eyes to find a pair of eyes staring back at me. In the dimly lit area they look almost luminous, but when I kneel, crawling over to her, I notice they're a strange green that seems to change as she moves her head, watching me.

"Who are you?" I ask, softly, knowing she's probably scared and freaked out. I was too when I first arrived here. This time though, I realize I'm no longer afraid, I'm angry. I always thought I was the only one. I was stupid enough to think he'd learned his lesson when I left. But she's proof that there's nothing for this vile monster to learn.

What needs to happen is he needs to be killed. One way or another, I'll find a way out of here and I'll make him pay. She watches me for a moment longer before stepping closer to the bars of her cage.

"I'm Ellie." She smiles. She's incredibly pretty. Young. The thought hurts my heart that she's in here when she should be out there living a normal life.

"Why are you here? How did he find you?" Her eyes brim with tears as she regards me and I'm afraid I've upset her more than I wanted to. She shakes her head, but watches me. "I was here a long time ago too. I escaped. We'll get out of here. I promise." My words feel foreign. Who am I to promise her anything. We're in this together. If I can keep her strong, willing to fight, then we'll get through it. Somehow.

"I..." she starts, but her voice breaks and the tears flow as she blinks. "I thought I was safe when he said he'd help me." Fury rages through me when I realize he gave her the same sordid story he gave me. Just then, the rattle of keys renders my body rigid with fear and when the door swings open, I am face to face with my tormentor. The monster.

"Little whore." He smirks, eyeing me ravenously.

He stalks into the room and straight for me. There's nowhere to go. I'm trapped once more and he's going to hurt me worse than I've ever been before. I know this because when I glance down he's carrying chains. Thick metal chains that dangle and clink loudly. Echoes hit the walls and attack my ears with vengeance.

I can't do this. Not again. I try to breathe but I can't. It's difficult. The suffocating attacks me viciously, gripping my throat and squeezing. Once the door to my cage is wrenched open, he reaches for me, gripping my arm painfully as he rips me from the safety of my prison.

"It's time I taught you a lesson on why little girls never run away from me," his tone thick with lust and filthy with sin. Nothing will stop this from happening. I'm too weak to fight, and he's too agile and alert to make a mistake.

He pulls me toward a chair, shoving me into the seat. Then he goes to work. His hands move quickly, binding my ankles to either of the chair legs. My hands are bound behind me, which causes my breasts to jut out. My body is on display, open for him to use and abuse as he wishes.

"You know, it was so easy to find you. Imagine my luck when I found you had given yourself to Elijah Draydon, the man I was watching for some time. Mainly because I knew he was the man from the hospital who had been visiting you," he tells me. Stalking around me, he continues. "You think it's real love? A man like him doesn't love, he fucks, and he'll break you, just as I will do now."

"You don't know anything about—"

His hand slams into my stomach causing me to retch, the puke burns its way up my throat as it falls from my mouth. "You never were an obedient slut," he hisses in my ear.

He then casts a glance behind him, toward the second cage. Ellie, the sweet girl is crying now. "You'll watch this, because if you ever try to leave, this is what will happen to you." He picks up a leather belt from the cabinet which houses torturous devices, and lifts it, bringing it down on my thighs. He rips sounds from me that are inhumane.

The leather burns, it stings. Cutting into the sensitive flesh of my inner thighs. Tears stream down my face in rivers of pain.

"You fucking little bitch, running away from me is something you'll never do again. Do you hear me?"

He grunts, it's feral and vile. He sounds maniacal as he spits his words. Suddenly, cold liquid is splashed on my thighs. "Whore." He utters with disgust. When I finally manage to open my eyes, I notice the red paint all over my body. It drips like rain from a rooftop.

My eyes glance over to Ellie, she's sobbing uncontrollably and all I can hope is that Carrick is on his way. That somehow, he's found out where I am because I'm no longer able to do anything. William stalks closer to me, he looks older than he did when I was here last. His hair is graying, and I know he's not older than forty.

He reaches for me and I feel the prick of a needle before I see it. Electricity races through my veins at an alarming rate and when I glance at him again, I notice how my vision blurs. I can't open my mouth, I feel lethargic and I wonder if he's drugged me to pass out. But then he brings something warm toward me. It sends a shudder through me.

"Do you like that feeling, whore? The heroin will slowly eat away at your restraint and make you pliable," he informs me. I open my mouth, but I'm not screaming anymore. There's no longer fear, just acceptance. I'm going to die. At least before my end, I loved someone. I gave Elijah all I had and I spent those final days happy.

A knife is pulled from somewhere, and glints in the dim light, as I watch the tip of the blade trail a line over my chest. A crimson trickle appears in the wake of the blade as he marks me. I can't tell from here what he's carving into my flesh, all I can feel is this overwhelming urge to cry, to scream. But my mind is no longer mine.

The trickle of blood tickles as it drips from the flesh that's torn. Just like me, I'm ripped apart. A toy that's no longer good for anything. My breathing is shallow as he drains me.

"You see, little Ellie, this is what happens to whores. You're not a whore, are you?" He sneers. My narrowed gaze is locked on him as he strolls over to the cage, unlocking it, and tugging the poor girl out. I'm afraid for her. I no longer care what he does to me. But she's innocent. She shouldn't be here.

He grips her breasts, tugging at the nipples, causing her to scream.

"Whore, do you hear that? She loves my touch, not like you. You're a filthy broken toy. Elijah Draydon will never want you." Once again, the words he pierces me with hurt worse than the wounds on my body.

He drags Ellie over to me, forcing her down on her knees. The drugs and the loss of blood, make me dizzy, but I try to focus on the girl. She gazes up at me with fear, trepidation and I wish that somehow, at least she will be saved.

"Take this," he tells her, shoving a knife in her hand. "Make her scream." His order is clear. He's wanting to torture me by using an innocent child.

"Fuck you," I spit. I'm weak, but I will fight till the end. His backhand slams into my jaw, causing me to lurch and the chair to topple. The chains dig into my flesh.

"Is that what you want?" he hisses. Gripping my hair, he pulls me and the chair up and I hear the sound that's haunted me for so long. A belt buckle, a zipper, and then my throat is full. I heave against the crown of his filthy cock that's shoved so deep down my throat I feel it pulse in my esophagus.

Tears blur Ellie as she whimpers on the floor, watching me get violated. Rather me than her. He continues to hurt me, to fuck my face so hard, I feel the bile rise in my stomach and up my throat. I retch violently as the burn of my vomit hits the cuts on my chest.

I close my eyes and go to another place. I go to Eli. I see him, I feel him. I allow him to bathe me in his comfort. And that's when everything goes black.

TWENTY THREE

ELIJAH

We're moving too slow. The plane is heading in to land and my body is alert, ready to murder, to maim, and to make sure that someone dies tonight. That someone in particular is a man I was supposed to be aiding. William Fredericks.

I'm still simmering quietly when Carrick glances up from his phone. His eyes have a way of confessing before he's even opened his mouth.

"What?"

"The signal on her phone is still on, we just need to hope that we don't lose it." Shoving from the seat, I settle beside Carrick and watch as a red dot appears and pulses in the middle of fucking nowhere. "We'll get her back," he assures me for about the hundredth time today, but deep down, I'm more fearful of what has been done to her. I don't think he'll kill her, but he will break her. Or try to.

"We will. But in what state?" I ask the question that's been weighing on my mind. Heavily. More so, it's gripped my heart. Painfully.

He doesn't answer me, because he can't. There's no way he can tell me with confidence that she'll be okay. That all this will be swept under the rug. The wheels touch down and I'm out of my seat, at the door waiting for clearance to open it.

This monster has stolen from her before. Her innocence, her trust, and her sanity. This time, I'm scared he'll steal her soul.

The doors slide open with a whoosh and I'm already down the steps and at the waiting car before Carrick has time to think. When he joins me, I'm in the bench seat of the town car. The driver glances back at us and nods. The GPS he has plugged in at the front of the car is beeping to the beat of my heart. It's a whisper, but I hear it.

I hear her. I feel her. If she were dead, I'd know. My

gaze is focused on the nothingness outside the window. It's black. Just like my heart and mind. Dark thoughts float through me, images of what we're about to discover taunt me and I can't help the ache in my gut. As if I've been punched, stabbed, a blade shoved so deep inside it's pierced my soul and every moment I'm away from her, I feel life drip from me.

Finally, as we round a bend, our driver, I don't know his name, pulls up against a high black wall in the middle of darkness.

"We're here. Let the team get in there and disarm everything. Then we'll enter from the rear," he says, his voice thick and filled with excitement at having to play soldier. His accent very much like Carrick's is English, and I realize that there's a lot more to Rick Anderson than meets the eye.

When we're alone, I glance at Carrick who pulls a 9mm from a holster and hands another one to me, which he had hidden on his right side.

"You never know when you need one," he shrugs, exiting the car before I can even mention it. Silence ensues as we wait. It's deadly. My mind is raging. Nothing is going to help me now, only holding my girl will ease this tension and rage.

Before I have time to think, it all happens. Swiftly, the lights that we agreed would be the signal flash and Carrick and I are on our feet racing toward the gate as it slides open. The forest is dark, dank, but then as the black metal gates open, we're met with the humongous fortress that is the Fredericks mansion.

I don't think. My mind is blank. No, that's a lie. It's on one thing, and she's inside. As soon as we reach the doors, we find it open, and the six men are inside with their guns drawn. I've never shot a gun, I've only ever been in a bar fight; this is something different altogether. There's nothing that could prepare me for walking into a house that looks like the queen lives there.

It's ornate, gilded, and I have the sudden urge to smash everything to pieces. I want to destroy anything and everything that belongs to this asshole.

"Basement. Basement." One of the men hisses into his earpiece. We follow the black figures as they make their way into the bowels of the house.

It's silent and fear grips me. *She can't be dead. She has*

to be alive. I can't live without her. I can't. These thoughts race through my mind as we head down the staircase to the cold basement, which looks like it should house corpses rather than a beautiful woman. And I hope and pray to a god I don't believe in that I won't find her corpse lying in that small room on the other side of the large metal door.

We're about to break the door in when I hear it. A scream.

"Gia!" I call out not thinking. Carrick's glare pins me and I know I fucked up. Another scream and I realize it's not her. It's not her voice. Something's wrong. *Who is that?*

I don't know how they get the door open, but with a loud resounding crash it moves and we're inside in seconds. Gunshots sound and ring in my ears and I fall to the floor. Pain so profound shoots through me. My leg is oozing blood from a bullet, but that is not what hurts, it's the woman on the floor that's chained to a chair. I don't know what's happening around me, loud screaming, shouting, more gunshots, but all I see is her.

Time stops. My breathing halts. And my body

freezes. She's not moving. Blood pools around her like she's bathing in it. I grip the floor, dragging myself toward her. Her chest doesn't rise and fall. I reach for her neck, but there's no pulse. There's no breaths.

A cry is ripped from my soul. As if someone had reached into my body and tore my very life force from me and I'm lying beside her dying. Not again. I can't lose another. I will never survive it.

"Get her into the fucking ambulance," Carrick shouts above me. Men grab at my woman. Her body is lifeless as they unchain and lift her from the floor. Rick helps me to my feet and I stumble beside him as we make our way out toward the main section of the house.

"Where—"

"He'll be taken care of until you're ready," Rick informs me, and I nod. *I'll be back for the fucker.* He can be sure I'll be coming for him. And the rest of his fucking family.

Once Carrick and I reach the car, I'm losing the feeling in my leg. But all I can think of is my girl.

"She's dead," I tell him but he shakes his head. "She had no pulse. No breathing. She's fucking dead!" I'm shouting, but I don't give a fuck. I'm angry. I'm broken. I can't do this. And I realize, for the first time in a long time. In years. I'm crying. I'm fucking bawling my eyes out and I don't care who sees me.

Women aren't the only ones to hurt. To shatter. And I realize it in that moment. I've just lost the love of my life. Again.

TWENTY FOUR

GIANA

Beep. Beep. Beep.

Hiss. Whoosh. Hiss. Whoosh.

Beep. Beep. Beep.

Hiss. Whoosh. Hiss. Whoosh.

The sounds calm me, but nothing stops the pain. My skin feels like it's on fire. I can't open my eyes and I'm not sure if it's from the medication they've put me on, or if it's from my injuries. Although, I don't know what I look like. I have no idea what my injuries are.

Beep. Beep. Beep.

Hiss. Whoosh. Hiss. Whoosh.

Beep. Beep. Beep.

Hiss. Whoosh. Hiss. Whoosh.

"Gia," his voice comes through the chorus of machines. I don't move. If I do, he'll know I'm awake. Then what? He'll pity me. He'll tell me he's sorry and loves me. But why? Because he feels guilty. That's why. No man would stay with me now. And I'm okay with that. I don't want a man near me. I never want to feel the touch of anyone. The thought alone causes me to cringe.

"Mr. Draydon, I just need to administer the medication," the nurse says quietly. "She'll wake up soon. You don't have to stay all the time." Her voice has a smile in it. Almost as if she's trying to placate him. To keep him calm from the storm I feel emanating from him.

"I'm not leaving her." And there it is. Guilt. It's so thick in his tone that I want to scream at him. Tell him it's not his fault. It's mine. Silence again. I hear the whoosh of the machines and I wonder if it's drugs that will numb me. I want to feel nothing. I want to die.

Would they give me an overdose if I begged?

"I'll be back to check her vitals again in an hour," the

nurse informs him. Silence settles, and I wonder if he's actually going to leave, but he doesn't. I feel his hand on me, I want to pull away, but I can't move. I'm bound. I'm burning. I hurt.

"You're a fucking little slut for running away from me. I was the one who took you in when your parents didn't want you." He hisses in my face. Dark eyes pierce me. They slice into my soul more than I ever believed he could. My flesh burns. The hot wax, mixed with the blood that drips from me is too much.

I beg. I cry. But it's no use.

He pushes me down, my body flat on the cold concrete. And then he's above me. He shoves his cock, hard and erect, into my body. I'm dry. It burns like acid. He grunts as he pulls out and shoves back inside me. Again, and again.

His hands on my throat squeeze hard, choking me as he violates me. "That's it, whore. Take me. You love it. Don't you? That's what you and he did. He fucked you rough. I've known you for too long. I know you love being used like a fuck toy."

He continues his assault. It rips me apart. My cervix feels like it's being crushed. I'm about to pass out from his

*fingers choking me, but I'm not that lucky. He releases me,
causing me to choke and cough.*

*As soon as I think I've earned a reprieve, he shoves three
fingers into my mouth. The tips open my throat which make
me gag and spit up bile. It burns, and tears form in my eyes. I
can't take anymore.*

Elijah. I love you.

*The words float from my heart, and I hope that they reach
him. And that's when I pass out.*

"I love you so much. I… I wish I'd gotten to you
earlier. Jesus, I can't lose you, Gia. Come back to me.
Please?" He pleads. Every day he does it. He sits there,
holding my hand, causing me to retch, and he begs. He
pleads for me, but I don't know if I can find it in myself
to ever let him back in. Not because I don't love him, but
because I do.

When the quiet comes, I sigh inwardly and then he's
on his feet and I realize I'm awake and he heard me. He
can hear me and I can't bring myself to tell him I don't
want him here. I no longer need Daddy to look after me.

"Gia? Can you hear me? Baby, are you there?" I don't

reply. No response means he may just move on. Maybe he'll finally get the idea of moving on. Of leaving the broken toy. "I'll never leave you, baby. I'm right here," he affirms and my heart sinks. I don't want him here. The only man I need is Carrick.

"Mr. Draydon, can we have a moment with Giana please?" That's when he finally leaves my hand, but he leans in. I feel his hot breath on me and normally, I'd want it. I'd need it, but not tonight. All I want is to be alone. No men. No one who can ever see me as broken. As shattered. And no one who can ever learn what I really am.

"You're awake, I know you are," the nurse tells me when Eli finally leaves my bedside and I'm alone for the first time in days. When I open my eyes, she's staring at me. "He loves you," she tells me in an almost angry grunt as she tugs on the pipes and machines that connect me to life. To this world.

"I love him too," I tell her earnestly. The only problem

is that I don't know how he'll ever want someone like me.

"Why don't you talk to him?" She asks the most practical question, but I can't answer because I don't know how. I love Eli more than life itself. He was the one who saved me, in more ways than he even knows.

"Sometimes, when you love someone, you have to let them go. And as much as it hurts." I cast a quick glance at her, then my eyes find the door again. I continue. "As many times, as that person promises forever, no human can guarantee it. I almost died. He's already lost someone he loves. I can't allow him to lose me. The problem is," I drag my stare over to hers. "Sometimes, no matter how much you're meant to be with someone, life steps in and breaks it apart anyway."

She watches me for a moment as if I've lost my mind. Perhaps I have. But in my head, I'm making sense. As much as I'm meant to be with Eli, life has fucked that and I can't ever let myself allow him to love me in that way. He can't lose me again, he can't watch another love of his life die. I heard him that night. I heard him utter those words and I vowed in my deliriousness I'll never be the source of his pain. I'll never be the one he loses.

"What if you don't have a choice?" the nurse asks me.

"Everyone has a choice. Get the doctor to sign my release documents. I need to go home. I can't be here anymore." This place is making me worse. I'm sick. I need help. And the only way to fix me is to get out of here and focus on a new life. Perhaps even a new city. If Carrick will help me, I'll be able to get out of here, let Eli live a life of happiness with another toy, and I can try to heal from my injuries.

"He'll never give up. Even after everything he's still here. Lovie, he's never going to give up on you. Mark my words." She words it ominously. But deep down, I don't doubt that Elijah will never let me go. No matter how I push, he'll pull. And like a puppet, I'll be tugged back by the strings that bind me to him.

"What are you doing, Gia?" I'm staring at Carrick across the room and I know why he's asking. Because there's a man outside the door that's waiting to talk to me. I've avoided him for six hours. It's a record for me, but now I'm caught and I have nowhere to run.

Savvie, Mason's submissive, is seated just beside me. Her hand on my leg, holding it steady from bouncing.

"Let him in," I say in a voice that isn't my own. The door slips wide and there he is. In all his six-foot glory, the man who still holds my heart.

"Why, sweet girl?" he questions. His voice is husky, filled with emotion I don't feel. I'm numb. Void of all emotion. I watch him stalk in and he stops just beside Carrick who's sitting on the sofa opposite me. It's far enough.

I can't move. Savvie's hand is the only thing anchoring me to this life. To the here and now.

"I need you to let me go, Eli," I plead, but he shakes his head.

"Never." His voice and tone are adamant. I'll never be free of him. Not that I want to be, but I want him to be happy. To live a life without the memories of me. Of my brokenness. I'm no longer the woman he loves. If he thinks that then he's sorely mistaken.

"Eli—"

"Listen to me, Giana, I fucking love you. I'll never love anyone the way I do you. If you think, for even one moment, I'll ever give up on you, then you're sorely fucking mistaken. I'll fight to the death to have you again. To put a ring on your finger, give you kids, a home, a family. And even if I manage that on my dying breath when I'm old and frail. I'll fucking do it." I don't doubt him. Hell, I believe him more than I do anything else in my life. Past or present. But, right now, I can't even stand being in the same room.

"Goodbye, Eli," my words are a soft whisper. Filled with emotion and yearning, pain and anguish, and as I push up from the chair, and walk toward the door, I feel him. He follows me. His hand on my arm sends anxiety spearing through me.

"This will never be goodbye," he bites out angrily. Not at me. Not at our situation. He's informing me that I'm fucked. He loves me and as much as I want him to move on, I'll never have that happen. He loves me too much.

"There's a problem when you love someone too

much, Eli. It can kill you." He watches me then. His eyes never leaving mine. I feel him respond. Instead of words. He offers me something more. So much more than I ever thought possible.

Then, a moment later, he nods. His gaze drops to the carpet and I find I miss it. Like the air I breathe, I need him. His eyes on me. His hands keeping me safe.

"Gia, I'm already dead."

And with that, he turns and walks away. He doesn't tell me to call. He no longer offers promises. All he gives me is the raw, honest truth. I may not have died, but I killed the only man who loved me.

"Goodbye, Eli."

And that's when I break down. My body crumples to the floor in sobs that wrack me inside out. Carrick is gone. Everyone is gone but Savvie and me. She is on the floor beside me in seconds and I let it all out. I let all the loss ooze from me. And I let go of Eli in my tears.

TWENTY FIVE

ELIJAH

It's been radio silence for days. I can't take it anymore. She said goodbye and I gave her that, but this is becoming ridiculous. I stalk into Sins to find a barman I don't recognize. Savvie and Ellie, the girl we saved from the cage is sitting beside her.

"Where is she?" I ask as soon as I reach the two girls.

"She's not here," Carrick's voice comes from behind me before either of the girls can respond. He stalks up to me and offers his hand, which I shake in greeting. "We have something to finish before you can even comprehend going to her."

I know what he's talking about. I still haven't had the courage to go near the fucker that stole my girl. I knew that if I walked up to him, I'd have ripped him to shreds. Granted, he would deserve it, but I can't sit in prison while Gia is out here alone.

"Let's go," Rick says, patting me on the shoulder. Without looking back, I follow him through the club and out into the parking lot.

"Just tell me if she's okay." My voice comes out filled with emotion I haven't felt in a long while. That absence of the person you love ensures that your life is void of color. The once red roses that Gia reminded me of are black as night in my mind.

"She will be. Time is all she needs right now. And you my friend," Carrick glances my way. "Need closure and vengeance for your girl."

Nodding, I slip into the passenger seat of a black BMW X5 that I've never seen him drive. The windows are blacked out, hiding us from the outside world. The engine purrs to life, my heart hammers in my chest at what I'm about to do. Beside killing him, the only way I'll find closure is to torture the fucker.

I'll gladly do that if it means my girl will find peace. Knowing he's gone will make sure her mind is at rest.

No longer stressed about him once again finding her.

As we travel through the darkened streets, I don't talk, I can't find words to thank Rick for what he's done. Nothing can ever compare to having friends who will have your back no matter what. He's become closer to me than any family I've had.

Fifteen minutes later, we're pulling up to an abandoned warehouse on the outskirts of town. It's derelict. The perfect place to kill someone and hide a body.

Once the car stops and the engine ceases, we sit in silence for a moment before Carrick pulls a black 9mm from his jacket.

"This is for you. I'm not saying you'll use it, but…" His words taper off into nothing and I know what he's saying. If I want to pull the trigger it's loaded and ready. I've never taken a life, never wanted to. Now that I grip the metal, I have the urge to empty the whole round in that asshole's chest. To see the blood drip from the bullet holes.

"Let's go," I utter gruffly. Pushing the door open, I exit the vehicle with the firearm firmly in my tense grip.

The crunch of our steps on the loose granite are the only sounds in the dead of night. Darkness envelops us, the sliver of the new moon offers only a small amount of light. "Did you lock him up in this place?"

"My men did, yes," Carrick answers. Mysterious. Not giving anything away about who he really is which makes me want to question him. To learn more about the man that seems to know people who have derelict warehouses on the outskirts of town where you can hold a hostage.

Once we step inside the barren space, I spot one chair with a slumped form in it. There aren't any other visible signs of the men Carrick mentioned. As we near the unconscious man, two figures dressed in black and carrying machine guns step forward from the shadows.

"Mr. Anderson, the hostage has been sleeping. Shall we wake him up?" one asks, facing Carrick. One nod from Rick, and the shadowed figure grips William Fredericks' hair, tugging it back.

"Wake up, asshole." The deep gruff voice vibrates through the warehouse.

When I get a better look, I notice he's roughed up,

but not as bad as I thought. Or not as bad as I want to hurt him. His eyes open; blood crusted in the corner of his mouth cracks when he smirks.

"Is that little whore alive?" he spits, causing me to rear back and slam the butt of the gun into his mouth. Two teeth fly from his lips, falling to the ground.

"Don't you speak about her like that you piece of filth." My words are hissed in his face, and spittle flies from my venomous mouth.

"She was a whore, you know? Her body was nothing but a device to gain pleasure from."

Rage warms my blood, it rushes through my veins like a poison, a drug. Lifting the gun, I trail the barrel over his bloodied face.

"You know, William... I have two bullets in here with your name on it. One for Gia and one for Ellie. All those times you hurt them, violated them, you will pay. I promise you that," I vow, dropping my hand to his crotch and pointing it at his stomach.

"You can't kill me, Elijah. You're too soft. In love. That emotion weakens you." His words have no effect on me. Nothing but hatred simmers in my gut for him.

"Oh, I'm not going to kill you," I tell him with a smirk. My finger presses the trigger easily. The shot resounds, and a cry is wretched from his throat. Blood splatters over my chest, my arm, and my hand. I'm drenched in the crimson liquid of the enemy. "That's for Ellie," I tell him, seeing the agony in his expression. The thing about it is I know exactly where to shoot to wound, but not kill.

"Just…" He gurgles. "Arrest me," he pleads. His voice drops to a whisper.

I've learned that words spat are meant to harm. When uttered, they're meant to console. But when they're whispered, that's when they mean so much more. The emotion so profound it chokes you, and all you can manage is a whisper. Whether it's passion, lust, agony, pain, or sorrow.

Lowering the gun further, right at the filthy cock that's hurt two women that I know of, but what worries me is the one's we weren't there to save, I once again pull the trigger. Lifting my eyes to the men in shadows, I nod.

"Take him to the hospital and call the police." Once

he gets into the emergency room they'll save him, and then he'll rot in prison for the rest of his life. Carrick's team works quickly, and I know they'll get him there on time. I watch as the blood drains from him and I can't help smiling. The sick satisfaction I feel only seems to make me happier. I wish I could've found him sooner, before he managed to steal Gia, or even Ellie. But now he'll get what's coming to him.

"You okay, man?" Rick asks from beside me, and I nod, handing him back his gun.

"I am. Time to move on. Wait for my girl to come back to me."

It doesn't take long for us to get back to the city. We do so in silence. Rick pulls into his parking spot at the club and I exit his car.

"Thank you for everything," I tell him, unlocking my own vehicle.

"You're welcome to come in for a drink you know," he says, pointing to the entrance. But I shake my head.

"Time to go home." I slip into the driver's seat and start the car. It's not long and I'm pulling into my garage. The house is empty, leaving another barren feeling in my chest. Pulling out my phone, I hit dial on her number. Gia.

"Hello," she says tentatively. It's the first time in days she's answered a call from me and my heart thunders in my chest.

"I miss you." It's the truth. I do. My heart aches. My body yearns for her. And she can't deny she feels the same.

"Please don't call me again. I've already said goodbye." She hangs up. The beep on the other end of the line is enough for me to want that gun of Carrick's to take the pain in my chest away.

Sighing, I head into the living room. I pour myself a triple shot of amber liquid, the whiskey that I keep for special occasions. Tonight, I might have won the war, but I lost the princess. And I know somehow, I have to come to terms with it.

EPILOGUE

GIANA

"Are you going to see him?" Savannah asks as she rounds the bar. Ellie and Peyton are sitting along the counter top watching me with both awe and pity. I hate it. Dragging my gaze away from the glass of vodka I'm nursing, I meet Savvie's big dark blue eyes. They remind me of an evening sky. And they twinkle like stars are hidden in them. Small blue gemstones. Lapis Lazuli.

"I can't." It's the only thing I've said for three months. Spending time away from Elijah has allowed me to think. After what happened, I couldn't bear him touching me. I couldn't even handle him looking at me. I know I hurt him when I walked away, but I just couldn't lead him on. Make him love me more when I wasn't sure that love is something I could ever do.

I don't blame him. It's the last thing I do. But deep down, all I remember is pain. The agony. My skin slowly healed over the last few months, but it's not the outer scars that hurt, it's the emotional scars. The inner turmoil.

Nightmares have returned full force. I've been at the psychologist office more than I've been at home. I might as well move in there. I had to get a new doctor. A woman. The only man who can even come within a few feet of me is Carrick.

"You know he'll never give up on you. Right?" Savvie says, the girls agree nodding their heads. Just then, our sweetheart walks in, Eva.

"Darlings," she smiles. Her eyes land on me and she sighs. She's seen Eli, I know he's been talking to Nate more than anything. I think Rick has been on Eli's shit list because he's allowed me back to work, and Nate has become his confidant. The three men, Oliver, Elijah, and Nate have been in the club while I work, but they don't allow Eli near me.

The first time he walked up to the bar, I lost it. My screech had alarmed the whole club. Carrick sent

Savannah and Eva to take me to his apartment and let me sleep it off.

"Eva, is he…?"

"He'll be in later. I think you should hear him out to be honest. He's been shattered, Gia. I've never seen any man in such a state. Just once. Even if you want us there. Allow him to talk to you. Please?" She watches me for a moment before I sigh.

I could try. "Will you and Sav be there?" She nods. "Okay, I'll try. I'm not promising anything, just… I just don't know how else to make this right."

"He loves you. There's nothing you need to make right. He's going to prove to you that you can be with him." She seems confident, which makes me smile. Something about this woman makes me smile. "Come here." She nudges her head to the side and reaches for my hand when I join her. "I have seen Nate's monster, I asked him for it and he broke me. I'm not saying it's the same. I could never understand the agony you're going through, but when a man loves you so truly, so honestly, you need to try. It may take time and that's okay. I know you love him." She smiles. It's a sweet, gentle one and I nod. It's true.

"I do."

"I know. That is why I need you to give this a chance. Don't let love go. If you do, you're letting that monster win. I know you're not doing it intentionally, but in a way, you're allowing him to rule your life."

"He is, I know he is," I tell her the truth.

"Then don't."

It's been three months and I'm still running. Still hiding. It's time to stop. Time to grow some lady balls and hopefully heal. I don't know how, or if it will work, but I know I'm going to try.

BONUS SCENE

ELIJAH

As soon as I walk into the room, I feel her. I've always known. Always been connected to her. Magnetized. But this time when I feel her, it's different. I know it because when my eyes meet hers, I realize it's not that long-lost love. It's not chemistry. It's nothing. There's nothing there. She regards me with a look that confirms it. It's over.

Strolling into the room, I notice Savvie sitting in the corner reading. I'm not sure where Mason is, but he's clearly losing his shit if he's letting her sit here and referee a match between Gia and me. I hold the dozen red roses out to her as I near her.

"You look pretty," I tell the woman who's still every

part of me as I am of her. Giana. She does look beautiful. A cute dress hugs her curves which has an intricate pattern of roses. A soft blush paints her cheeks and I wish, ache even, to see that blush on her ass. Shaking my head, I stalk closer, finding a seat in one of the many chairs dotted around the room.

"Thank you for coming," she says, as if I'm a fucking stranger. I don't reply immediately. Perhaps I'm an asshole, but I'm angry. Not at her, but at our situation.

"Why wouldn't I?"

"Look, I needed—"

"No, this is my time. I'm here because you pushed me away and I accepted it. I allowed you time off. I gave you everything you ever wanted and now, now it's time for what I want. I love you, Gia. I'll never stop fucking loving you. So it's time you realize that as many times as you push me away, all the times you force me to choose between coming here and stalking you or staying home sniffing the clothes you left behind, I'll always be here. No matter what."

And I mean it. In all my brutal fucking honesty I mean it.

"I want to give you everything. A family, a home, kids, a dog, a cat, whatever the fuck you want, Gia. Just let me in. Give me one fucking chance to prove I love you. To make you see I'm no monster. I'm yours. As you are mine."

I watch her for a moment. Only one second before she's in my arms. The pain that's been holding us both hostage for months falls away. We've kept it, held on to it. It's become a goddamn security blanket, but she no longer needs it because I'm here. I think she needed it to keep herself safe. That's when it happens. Her eyes tell me the truth. She finally says it.

Her lips part and the words tumble between us.

She takes the chance.

She confesses it.

She whispers, "I love you, forever."

"As I love you, Gia," I whisper in return.

PLAYLIST

- Take Me To Church - Hozier
- Beast Within - In This Moment
- It's Not Over - Daughter
- Better than Me - Hinder
- Ride - Chase Rice
- Whisper - Chase Rice
- Hello - Adele
- Hurricane - Thirty Seconds To Mars
- Passenger Side - Jay Sean
- Roulette - Katy Perry
- Let Her Go - Passenger
- Earned it - The Weeknd
- Hate It When You See Me Cry - Halestorm
- Bottoms Up - Brantley Gilbert
- A Thousand Years - Christina Perri

ACKNOWLEDGMENTS

This book was an idea a long while ago and as it morphed in my mind, it turned into Whisper, book two of the Sins of Seven Series. Elijah and Giana have had one crazy ride. They burrowed themselves in my heart and I can't believe you're holding them in your hands. It's not an easy feat getting a book ready for you, but I love every step of the journey.

I want to thank my beautiful BETA ladies who took the story, broke it apart and helped me polish it, Sheena, Melissa, Cat, and Joy, thank you for loving Eli and Gia as much as I do.

To my amazing editor, Shana, you are a diamond. I love you so hard for all you do for me. Thank you for falling for Eli and Gia and ensuring they're polished to perfection for me.

My PA, Michelle who puts up with all my demands, thank you babe ;) I know you love me really. Right? LOL! Thank you for all you do.

To my Cinders, thank you for taking on a supporting role in my journey, you're appreciated. Lots of love, girl! <3

My Dolls street team, thank you for always being there and supporting me. You ladies humble me with the love you show me. Tre, Sheena, Sarah, Susan, Tam, Lisa, TJ, Dawn, thank you again!

My Darklings, my beautiful reader group, you are my sanity in this crazy world. I know I'm never alone with you lot keeping me entertained. If I'm feeling down, you ladies cheer me up. Thank you for being amazing!

Lastly, my Captives, my review team, thank you for being my prisoners. As much as I do torture you with some of my storylines, you're still there, willing and able to read and review. Thank you!!

To all my author colleagues, thank you for always sharing, commenting, and supporting me. I appreciate every one of you. Having a support system is important and you ladies provide that and so much more. I'm always humbled by the incredible support from each one of you.

To ALL the readers and bloggers, from the bottom of my little black heart, THANK YOU. All you do for us authors is incredible. Reading and reviewing is demanding on your own time and you do it with a smile. Thank you so, so much. You are valued and appreciated for taking time out to show us so much love. #AllBlogsMatter #AllReadersMatter

If you enjoyed this story, please consider leaving a review. I'd love you forever. (Even though I already do!)

SINS OF SEVEN

READ MORE ABOUT THE OTHER COUPLES IN THE SERIES

ABOUT DANI

Dani is a USA Today Bestselling Author of dark and deviant romance with a seductive edge.

Originally from Cape Town, South Africa, she now lives in the UK where she explores old buildings and cemeteries while plotting her next book.

When she's not writing, she can be found binge-watching the latest TV series, or working on graphic design either for herself, or other indie authors.

She enjoys reading books about handsome villains and feisty heroines, mostly dark, always seductive, and sometimes depraved. She has a healthy addiction to tattoos, coffee, and ice cream.

You can find more information on her website, www.danirene. com, or find her on social media, Instagram and Facebook being her favorites. Along with her newsletter, which you can sign up for here - https://bit.ly/DaniVIPs

www.danirene.com

info@danirene.com

FIND DANI ONLINE

Do you follow me?
If not, head over to any of the below links,
I love to hear from my readers!

Amazon

BookBub

Facebook

Facebook Group

Goodreads

Twitter

Pinterest

Instagram

Website & Store

Newsletter

Spotify

OTHER BOOKS

Find all my books online by visiting my website

www.danirene.com

or find my books on all major retailers - Amazon, Apple Books, Kobo, Barnes & Noble, Google Play, as well as the Kiss reading app, or Radish

Printed in Great Britain
by Amazon

24352778R00187